"You ____ ____
"I w____ ____ ____

Luca dragged in a breath then threw his head back and laughed. His initial reaction had been one of shock; he wasn't used to anyone refusing him something he wanted. But now that he was over his initial surprise he felt a wave of excitement ride his spine. He loved a challenge, and Morgan was proving to be a challenge in more ways than one.

She was a beacon of defiance, resisting him at every turn. It had been a long time since a woman had done that. Usually all he had to do was crook his little finger to have whatever woman he wanted come running.

The thrill of the chase set his insides buzzing until it was all he could do to sit still.

He would win in the end, of course. He always did.

But this time he had the feeling the journey would be half the fun.

"You're just dragging this out, you know," he murmured. "As I told you last night, I always get what I want."

TINA DUNCAN lives in trendy inner-city Sydney with her partner, Edy. With a background in marketing and event mangement, she now spends her days running a business with Edy. She's a multitasking expert. When she's not busy typing up quotes and processing invoices, she's writing. She loves being physically active and enjoys tennis (both watching and playing), bushwalking and dancing. Spending quality time with her family and friends also rates high on her priority list. She has a weakness for good food and fine wine and has a sweet tooth she has to keep under control.

DA SILVA'S MISTRESS

TINA DUNCAN

~ MISTRESS BRIDES ~

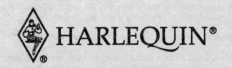

TORONTO • NEW YORK • LONDON
AMSTERDAM • PARIS • SYDNEY • HAMBURG
STOCKHOLM • ATHENS • TOKYO • MILAN • MADRID
PRAGUE • WARSAW • BUDAPEST • AUCKLAND

Recycling programs
for this product may
not exist in your area.

ISBN-13: 978-0-373-52750-2

DA SILVA'S MISTRESS

First North American Publication 2010.

Copyright © 2009 by Tina Duncan.

www.eHarlequin.com

Printed in U.S.A.

DA SILVA'S MISTRESS

CHAPTER ONE

IT WAS DONE.

Or at least it was as good as done.

The requisite phone calls had been made and instructions given. Gino had been despatched to collect the Marshall woman and bring her back here to the London headquarters of Da Silva Chocolate.

She had no idea what was about to hit her.

No doubt she thought her precious Joseph was behind her unexpected summons.

Instead *he* would be waiting for her.

Luca smiled grimly.

Within the hour it would all be over.

Within the hour Morgan Marshall would discover just how stupid she'd been to mess with the da Silva family.

Luca swung the black leather chair back to his borrowed desk and picked up the latest quarterly figures for the chocolate division of his vast empire, pushing the whole ugly incident with the Marshall woman to the back of his mind.

She would be here soon enough. He would say his

piece and then throw her out on the street where she belonged.

She wouldn't bother him or his family again; he'd make sure of it.

Twenty minutes later Luca was still poring over the report, this time with a frown, when someone knocked on the door.

'Enter!' he said, without looking up.

He heard the door open, but continued circling some numbers he wasn't happy with. When he was done, Luca closed the folder, tossed down his pen and looked up.

His heart stopped.

The breath locked tight in his lungs.

Standing in front of the burly figure of Gino was one of the most beautiful women he'd ever seen. Tall and slender, with raven black hair swirling around her shoulders, she had an elegant face totally belied by the I'm-in-charge black leather boots encasing her calves.

Luca exhaled slowly, staring at her through narrowed eyes.

This was the she-devil threatening his sister's marriage?

This was the heartless and conniving witch who had seduced his brother-in-law?

She wasn't what he'd been expecting at all.

In Luca's opinion, a callous marriage-wrecker should look hard and calculating. Not young—she couldn't be more than twenty-two or three—and gifted with an intriguing mixture of innocence and sensuality that even he, a connoisseur of some of the most beautiful women in the world, couldn't help but appreciate.

Just by looking at her, Luca could tell that Morgan Marshall was way, *way* out of Joseph's league.

He was much more her type.

He knew how to handle a beauty like this.

Luca put a brake on his thoughts. There was only one way he was going to *handle* Morgan Marshall—and that was by teaching her a lesson she'd never forget!

'*You're* Morgan Marshall?' he asked, needing to be sure.

The woman angled her chin into the air in a gesture Luca found vaguely familiar. 'Yes. I'm Morgan Marshall.' She looked around, then pinned him with the most incredible black eyes. 'Where's Joseph?'

The blood turned to ice in his veins. She was so eager to see her lover. Would she feel the same way after he'd finished with her? Somehow Luca doubted it.

Ignoring her question about Joseph's whereabouts, he asked, 'Do you know who I am?'

She nodded. 'You're Luca da Silva.'

'That's right. Joseph's brother-in-law.'

She didn't say anything to that.

He could imagine why.

'Are you aware of that?' he pressed.

Her eyes remained steady on his but Luca sensed her sudden tension. 'Yes. Joseph is married to your sister, Stefania.'

Although he'd half expected it, her answer still disappointed him. For a second—just one—he'd hoped there had been some terrible misunderstanding. That maybe she hadn't known Joseph was married. That perhaps Joseph had kept that information to himself.

Instead he had confirmation of her culpability.

Rather than re-igniting his anger, as it should have done, her response left him feeling strangely flat and out of sorts.

Because he wanted to pursue her himself?

The answer came quick as a flash: *yes!*

Given the right circumstances, that was exactly what he would do.

Only the right circumstances didn't exist—and never would.

He had to face the ugly truth.

Morgan Marshall had known exactly what she was doing when she'd slept with Joseph. She hadn't accidentally found herself in bed with a married man. She'd gone into the affair with her eyes open.

Now she had to face the consequences.

'Do you know why I brought you here?' he asked softly.

'No. I don't.' Eyes as dark as his own glinted with angry fire. She jerked her head to where Gino was standing squarely in the doorway behind her, barring any opportunity for her to escape. 'This…this…gorilla wouldn't tell me a damned thing. He barely speaks a word of English. Every time I asked him a question, he just grunted.'

'Did he, now?' *Good on you, Gino,* Luca thought, looking into Gino's impassive face. He'd instructed his head of security to say as little as possible when he collected her, wanting his involvement to come as a surprise. Judging by the wary look on Morgan Marshall's face, he'd more than succeeded in that endeavour.

'Yes. He did.' She thrust her hands onto slender hips. 'I told him it wasn't convenient for me to come with him, but he ignored me. He marched me out to the car as if I was some kind of criminal.'

'Did he hurt you?' Luca felt compelled to ask. Although he detested Morgan Marshall for sleeping with Joseph—how could he not, when he'd experienced first-hand the pain and destruction caused by extra-marital affairs?—he didn't condone violence against women under any circumstances. If she'd been a man, a good beating would be no more than she deserved. But then, if she'd been a man the situation wouldn't have arisen in the first place!

'No. But that's not the point.'

'Then what is?'

She gave him a look down the chiselled length of her nose that suggested he was several brain cells short of the full quid. 'The point is my being here is totally inconvenient. I have—*had*—a full schedule of appointments lined up for today. I had to ask my secretary to cancel them at the last moment.'

Luca inclined his head. 'That's regrettable, but unavoidable.'

'Is it? Maybe it's time you told me what this is all about. And while you're at it, why don't you tell me where Joseph is? This is his office. You shouldn't be in here without him.'

Luca stared at her in amazement. She was like a miniature firecracker going off, eyes glittering, so much energy vibrating off her, he expected to see sparks fly from the ends of her hair at any moment.

Would she be as passionate in bed?

His eyes dropped to the thrusting swell of her breasts, clearly outlined beneath the black and white striped shirt she was wearing under her snappy black business suit.

She would be dynamite in bed.

How he knew that for certain, he wasn't sure, but know it he did.

Heat drip-fed into his blood stream, warming him from the inside out. He imagined taking her right now.

On the desk. Naked except for those sexy black boots wrapped tightly around his hips.

His body surged on such a powerful wave of lust that Luca almost put thought into action. Instead, with a frown, he dragged his eyes back to her face, sucked in a lung full of much needed air and thrust the thought aside.

Morgan Marshall was the last woman on earth he should be thinking about in *that* way.

'I intend making a formal complaint,' Morgan continued, eyes still blazing.

'Do you, now?' Luca drawled.

'Yes, I do. Joseph will be very angry when he hears how you've treated me.'

No doubt Joseph would be—if he ever found out about this meeting.

Rising to his feet, Luca rounded the desk. 'Leave us,' he ordered Gino.

Gino backed out of the room and closed the door behind him with a soft click.

'Joseph isn't going to hear about this meeting because you're not going to tell him.'

She blinked up at him. 'Of course I'm going to tell him.'

Luca took her arm and urged her across the room. 'No, you're not.'

Her perfume, something soft and spicy with a hint of orange, closed around him.

She licked her lips. 'I'm...I'm not?'

'No, you're not.' He eased her down onto one of two leather visitors' chairs. Then, instead of resuming his own seat, he leant his hips against the edge of the desk. 'Not if you know what's good for you.'

His words, accompanied by underlying steel, made her eyes widen. 'What...what's this all about?'

He smiled his most charming smile and watched as she blinked under the impact. 'Come on, Ms Marshall. You're a bright young woman. Surely you must have some idea.'

She stared up at him, her eyes deep, dark pools of confusion then angled her chin into the air. The gesture once again struck him as familiar. 'No. I have no idea. Unless there's a business matter you want to discuss with me.'

His hands clenched. The only 'business' he wanted to discuss with her was the *monkey business* she'd been up to with Joseph!

'Not as such, no. My business interests are extensive. I don't have time to involve myself in the day-to-day running of my companies. I have competent managers to do that.'

'Then what *do* you want to talk to me about?' Morgan asked, in a voice that had the faintest tremor running through it.

'Can't you guess?'

Her chin angled back into the air. It was a look Luca was becoming increasingly familiar with and equally ir-ritated by—because he couldn't figure out who she reminded him of.

'Why don't you spit it out, Mr da Silva? If you have something to say, just say it.'

Luca had to admire her spirit. She had guts. He'd say that for her.

It was just a shame she didn't have the morals to go with it.

He shifted position on the desk and was aware of her quick appraisal. He leaned forward, inhaling the tangy scent of citrus. 'I brought you here because I am termi-nating your employment with Enigma Marketing.'

She gasped. Swayed in her seat. Paled until even her mouth looked parchment white and her eyes blacker than black. 'You can't do that!'

'I certainly can.'

Normally such a blatant misuse of power would be abhorrent to him. But these were exceptional circumstances that required drastic action.

'You may own half the world, Mr da Silva, but you *don't* own Enigma Marketing. You have no say over who they employ or don't employ.'

He smiled with genuine amusement. 'Surely you can't be that naïve? One phone call was all it took to seal your fate.'

She gasped again, her eyes so wide they looked like saucers. 'I don't believe you. My boss wouldn't do that to me!'

'No?' He leaned closer. 'Not even if I threatened to take away the Da Silva Chocolate account from her agency?'

A deathly silence fell. The look on her face told him Morgan knew the answer to that question as well as he did.

Da Silva had done for chocolate what Versace had done for fashion. The brand had developed a cult following among chocoholics, connoisseurs and A-listers around the world, their exclusive lines *de rigueur* on the tables of the rich and famous.

Da Silva was the marketing agency's flagship account. Losing it meant losing jobs, not to mention reputation and the kudos that came from being associated with the brand.

And Enigma's CEO, Dawn Merchant, would do just about anything to stop that from happening.

He reached across to the corner of the desk and slid

the phone towards her. 'Why don't you call her? I'm sure Dawn will be happy to confirm what I've told you.'

Morgan looked from the phone to his face and back again. 'OK. I believe you. But you'd better have a damned good reason for firing me or I'm going to sue the pants off you!'

Luca almost laughed in her face. Almost. Except there was nothing funny about the way she was trying to tear apart his sister's marriage—particularly at a time when Stefania was so vulnerable.

His sister was battling depression over her inability to conceive. Although she was trying to put on a brave face and maintain a positive attitude, her failure to fall pregnant after the last IVF treatment had really knocked the stuffing out of her.

The last thing she needed right now was to discover the husband she adored was having an affair!

Luca was determined she would never find out.

It was because of him that Stefania was in this predicament in the first place. If only he'd—

Luca slammed a lid shut on his thoughts. He'd been through enough what-ifs and if-onlys to last him a lifetime. He'd almost driven himself crazy imagining what he could have done differently to avert the accident that had changed their lives.

But that was in the past. It was the present and the future that concerned him now. While he couldn't do anything about Stefania's infertility, he sure as hell could do something about Morgan Marshall.

'I could say it's because you're incompetent...but I won't,' he bit out harshly.

'Good,' she said hotly, eyes glinting. 'Because you'd

be wrong. I'm good at what I do. *Very* good! Dawn must have told you that.'

He inclined his head. 'If it's any consolation, she did.'

In fact Luca had been surprised by just how rigorously Dawn had defended her employee. When he'd first called her, he'd phrased his request as exactly that. A request. When she'd rattled off what seemed to him to be an inordinately long list of qualifications and skills, he'd turned the request into an order.

An order Dawn had continued to resist.

Morgan was a model employee.

She was an excellent team player.

Not to mention innovative and creative.

Luca had frowned at the phone as he'd listened.

Were they talking about the same woman? he'd wondered.

The paragon Dawn was describing hardly sounded like the type of woman to have an affair with a married man. But then, he'd reasoned, just because she was a capable professional it didn't mean she couldn't also have the morals of an alley-cat!

'It's no consolation and you know it!' Morgan glared up at him, her eyes glittering like black diamonds. 'Now, tell me why you fired me, and make it good—or I'll have my solicitor here before you can say Jack Robinson!'

Luca couldn't help but admire her spirit. At the same time her continued refusal to admit the truth hardened his heart, until it felt as if it was encased in a block of ice.

He put his face close to hers, watched her draw back in her chair. Then he said softly, 'I think your relationship with Joseph Langdon is reason enough, don't you?'

* * *

Morgan's world tilted on its axis. The blood drained from her head so quickly a series of black dots began swimming in front of her eyes.

She'd suspected something was wrong from the minute she'd walked through the door and found Luca da Silva waiting for her.

But not this.

He knew!

Somehow, Luca da Silva *knew.*

A wave of panic engulfed her. She couldn't breathe—as if a band of steel had been strapped around her chest and tightened until it hurt. Her palms grew sweaty. Her heart was pounding so fiercely she was surprised he couldn't hear it.

She dragged in a deep breath, and then another. Closed her eyes. Opened them again. And found herself looking at the hard shafts of his thighs. Her pulse quickened and heat stirred low in her pelvis. Swallowing, she dragged her gaze away.

How could this have happened?

They'd been so careful to keep their relationship a secret.

They always met in out-of-the-way places or in the privacy of her apartment. They'd even met here, in this very office, sometimes on genuine business matters but as often as not on the pretext of business just so they could see each other.

But it seemed they hadn't been careful enough.

Stomach churning, Morgan clenched her hands tightly together in her lap and angled her chin into the air. 'I don't know what you're talking about.'

He moved closer, until his face was inches from hers, his breath feathering her face. 'I'm-talking-about-your-relationship-with-Joseph-Langdon,' he bit out, his accent, barely noticeable until now, thickening.

'What about it?' She wanted to draw away from him. This close, she could smell the spicy scent of his shampoo, could feel the heat radiating off his skin. Her tummy muscles contracted on a wave of awareness that made her press her knees together. 'We're business colleagues.'

His head went back, nostrils flaring. 'You are *not* just business colleagues.'

Morgan resisted the urge to swallow. 'Says who?'

'Says me.'

Morgan looked away, her eyes following the strong column of his throat to the broad expanse of his chest. Just how much did he know? she wondered, fascinated by the ripple of muscle she could see beneath his shirt as he clenched his hands into fists.

Enough, she supposed, to drag her halfway across London to have this conversation!

Which meant she couldn't plead total innocence...

She lifted her head. 'We're friends, too. Is that what you want me to say? There's no law against that, is there?'

She didn't need to be a genius to understand that the string of Italian that followed wasn't in the least complimentary.

'We are,' she insisted.

'Really?' He pulled back from her with a jerk, as if breathing the same air she did somehow contaminated him. 'I don't think so.'

God, but the man was arrogant. He was barely listening to a word she said. Joseph had complained of that very thing so many times Morgan had lost count.

It was bad enough that Luca constantly intervened in

the running of Da Silva Chocolate, but what Joseph found completely untenable was Luca's interference in his marriage.

Talk about being over-protective. Luca was so busy handing out advice and looking after his sister's interests, he left no room for Joseph to be the kind of husband he wanted to be.

Well, she had no intention of sitting back and letting Luca walk all over her. She tossed her head, sending her hair swirling around her shoulders. 'Believe what you like! I don't care. You can't have me fired without good reason!'

He stilled. It was an incredible thing to watch. He looked like a lion when it first scented its prey. His body stiffened and the eyes that met hers were so cold she shivered.

'You think not?' Suddenly he levered himself away from the desk, walked around to the other side and sat down.

Morgan felt some of the tension drain out of her. His close proximity had put her on edge in more ways than one. Whether she liked it or not, Luca…affected her.

Made her aware of him as a man.

Made her aware of herself as a woman.

The thought horrified her.

Luca da Silva was the *last* person she should be thinking about in *that* way!

But somehow she couldn't help herself.

He was wickedly handsome. Hair as black as her own. Eyes as dark as her own. His body a patchwork of tightly honed muscle and warm golden skin.

But it was more than that.

She'd heard about people who had the kind of

charisma that turned heads, but she'd never met one of them…until now.

Luca had that indescribable something in spades.

Leaning back in his chair, Luca smiled. It was the kind of smile a shark might give before gobbling up much smaller prey. 'I want your promise not to see Joseph again.'

Her heart wrenched, her throat clogging with emotion.

Her lost job was forgotten—at least for the time being.

Time enough later to figure out how she was going to pay off her student loans and her mortgage without a job.

This—Joseph—was much more important.

He was the only family she had. The only person who'd ever really cared about her. Even her own mother had regretted her existence. Sheila had taken every opportunity to remind her daughter about how her conception had ruined her life.

Joseph was the exact opposite. He'd welcomed her with open arms, his delight so effusive she'd actually cried. For the first time in her life, she felt wanted. Really wanted.

And Luca was asking her to turn her back on that?

An invisible hand clenched around her heart, squeezing until it was a physical pain. She couldn't give Joseph up—couldn't give up the sense of belonging she'd felt since finding him after her mother died.

But she couldn't explain any of that to Luca.

Couldn't…because she'd promised Joseph she wouldn't discuss the true nature of their relationship with anyone.

So what did she do now?

She could tell Luca to go to hell, of course. It was on the tip of her tongue to do exactly that. But she had to be cautious. Antagonising him could make the situation worse—although how that was possible she wasn't quite sure.

Her other option was to lie.

She didn't want to. Lies and secrets had a terrible way of biting you on the backside when you least expected it.

But what other choice did she have?

Dragging in a deep breath, she looked across the desk at Luca and tried to smile. 'OK. I promise.'

'Liar.'

Her heart jerked in her chest, her cheeks burned and her attempt at a smile crumbled. 'I—' she started, but he cut her off with a dismissive wave of his hand.

'Don't bother.' He steepled his fingers beneath his chin, staring grim-faced over the top of them. 'I had hoped losing your job would be enough incentive to show you I mean business. But obviously you need a little more…encouragement to stay away from Joseph.'

Ice slid down her spine. How could he make such a simple statement sound so threatening?

He pulled open the top drawer and extracted something which he tossed down in the middle of the desk.

'What's that?' she croaked, staring at the rectangular piece of paper.

He leant back in his chair. 'Why don't you look for yourself?'

Shifting to the front of her seat, Morgan reached out and picked it up by the edge, as if it might bite. She looked down. It was a cheque. A cheque made out in her name for the sum of fifty thousand pounds.

Her fingers started to shake, her insides shrinking. She looked up, the blood draining from her head and settling like a dead weight in the pit of her stomach. Then she jumped to her feet and, with a vicious flick of the wrist, flung the cheque at his face. 'Don't be insulting!'

With lightning-quick reflexes he caught the wedge of paper in mid-air. 'Isn't it enough?'

Her breath caught, the insult catching her on the raw. Furious, she slammed her hands palms-down on the top of the desk and bent towards him. 'Do you really think you can *bribe* me to stay away from Joseph?'

'Yes!'

She shook her head. 'Well, you're wrong. Friends don't come with a price tag attached—nor do they come with a dispose-by date.'

He shrugged. 'It's a lot of money.'

It *was* a lot of money. Money she could no doubt do with now she was out of a job.

Four years at Oxford University had been expensive. Although she'd worked part-time—waitressing initially, followed by a stint as a marketing assistant—it hadn't been enough to cover her fees, books and general living expenses.

She'd had to borrow money to get through.

Fifty thousand pounds would wipe out her student loans, plus provide enough for her to live on and make her mortgage payments for the next few months while she looked for a new job.

But, while the money would be a godsend, Morgan wasn't in the least tempted to take it.

The price was too high.

Much too high.

Joseph and her self respect meant a hell of a lot more to her than any amount of money ever could.

'I don't care how much it is,' she said forcefully. 'I don't want it.'

He frowned, as if her response bothered him in some way. Then his expression changed and he rose to his feet and mimicked her position on the desk.

Their faces were so close, Morgan could smell the clean male smell of him, could see the flecks of gold in the darkness of his gaze. Her eyes settled on his mouth and suddenly she wondered what it would be like to kiss him.

The thought made her move sharply back from the desk.

'Everyone has a price. What's yours?' Luca asked, in a voice that grated like sandpaper down her spine.

'I don't have one.'

'No? We'll see. When Joseph comes back to London you won't be seeing him again. And that's a promise.'

Seemingly satisfied by her stunned silence, Luca sat down, pulled a folder towards him and began to read.

Morgan stared at the dark pelt of his hair, not quite sure what to say. Or do. She'd heard every word he said but only two had registered.

As if he sensed her gaze on him, Luca looked up, his eyes like black chips of ice. 'What are you still doing here? This conversation is over.'

'But—'

'But nothing. Now get out. Or do I have to get Security to throw you out?'

Although Morgan knew she was being foolish, she couldn't go just yet. She had to ask him something first. Dragging in a deep breath for courage, she asked quietly, 'Back from where?'

Luca's head shot up so fast she was surprised he hadn't pulled a muscle. 'What did you say?'

She swallowed. He looked dark and dangerous. But she didn't care.

Joseph had said nothing about a trip. That was unusual in itself. He always called her before he went away. Given the way Luca had confronted her, she was worried he'd said something to Joseph.

She gripped her hands tightly together in front of her, a ball of anxiety wedged firmly in the back of her throat.

Joseph had been suffering from chest pains for the last few months. He hadn't told anyone…except her. He refused to see a doctor, convinced the episodes were the result of stress.

If Luca had confronted him…

She shuddered to think what could have happened. Barely daring to breathe, she said tightly, 'Just tell me where Joseph is and that he's all right.'

It was like waving a red flag at an already angry bull. Luca went berserk, rounding the desk so fast her head spun. He grabbed her shoulders and dragged her close.

He put his face close to hers, lips curled into a snarl. 'You have no right to ask such questions! *Dio*! Don't you get it?' His hands tightened on her shoulders. 'Joseph Langdon is dead as—'

His words hit Morgan like a sledgehammer, each syllable an individual blow she felt right through to her bones. She swayed on her feet as the floor rose up to meet her. Luca's face, fuzzy around the edges, was the last thing she saw as she slid into a dead faint, completely unaware of the stunned expression that crossed Luca's face as he caught her before she hit the floor.

CHAPTER TWO

LUCA TENSED AS Morgan's long, sooty lashes fluttered. Good, she was coming round. She'd scared the life out of him when her eyes had rolled back in her head and she'd slid into a dead faint. He was only thankful he'd managed to catch her before she'd fallen and hurt herself.

She whimpered as if she was in pain, then mumbled something under her breath. Luca moved closer.

The scent of orange invaded his nostrils again. He drew back, just far enough to stare into her unconscious face.

She really was magnificent. Skin the colour of magnolia petals. Silky hair the colour of a raven's wing spread like a glimmering halo against the cushion he'd tucked under her head. A mouth that, while slightly too wide, had a sensually full lower lip that just begged to be kissed.

She stirred on the leather couch he'd laid her down on, lashes flickering.

'Joseph,' she muttered.

Luca jerked away from her as if he'd been burned, his stomach muscles contracting into a tight ball.

There was no mistaking what he'd heard this time. He'd been close enough to hear every damning syllable.

How dared she wake up with Joseph's name on her lips?

Fury rose up inside him like a two-headed monster. He could feel it bubbling away inside him.

One part of his brain recognised that his outrage was way out of all proportion, but another part of him, a far more primitive part, accepted the emotion for what it was.

Jealousy.

As crazy as it sounded, he was jealous of his brother-in-law.

His hands balled into fists as he stared into Morgan's face.

It was *his* name he wanted on her lips when she wakened.

It was *his* name he wanted her to cry out in the throes of passion.

Her lashes fluttered open. Eyes shadowed with pain gradually refocussed on his face. She stared at him for a long moment, awareness pulsing in the air between them, then swung her boot-clad feet to the floor, pushing him out of the way in the process.

She touched a hand to her forehead and frowned. 'You said…' She stopped and dragged in a breath. 'You said that Joseph was dead.'

Luca grew still, his insides clenching down hard.

The emotions etched on her face were genuine. He would bet a million pounds on it.

Morgan Marshall genuinely cared for Joseph.

Rising abruptly to his feet, Luca strode over to the window and stared out. The pale milky sunshine that had been struggling to warm the morning had finally given up, hiding behind a bank of metallic grey clouds.

The change in the weather suited his mood.

He resented Morgan's feelings for Joseph. He also recognised that persuading her to leave Joseph alone could prove more difficult than he'd first thought.

Not that her feelings changed anything.

Luca was determined nothing would affect the outcome of their meeting. Stefania was his number one priority. The affair had to end.

But he couldn't let her go on thinking Joseph was dead.

He wasn't that cruel.

'Joseph is alive and well and currently on my private jet on his way to Sydney, Australia, for a well-earned holiday with my sister,' he said, without turning from the window.

The silence that filled the room had an eerie quality to it. The hairs on the back of his neck prickled. A warning flash of movement reflected in the glass window made him spin on his heels just in time to ward off the blow Morgan had aimed at his head.

In one smooth motion, he twisted her arm behind her back and pulled her up close against him.

'You bastard!' she spat. 'Did you enjoy lying to me like that?'

Once again she reminded him of a firecracker going off. The energy emanating from her was powerful. She was so full of life-force she made every other woman he'd ever known pale in comparison.

And just like that, the wanting was back.

A surge of lust threatened to kick his legs out from under him. Her body was plastered against his, the cushioning softness of her breasts pushing against his chest, the warmth of her hips cradling his sex.

He dragged in a breath and forced himself not to act on the hormones raging through his system. 'I didn't lie,' he replied calmly. 'You passed out before I could finish my sentence. What I was going to say is that Joseph is dead as far as *you* are concerned.'

She just stared at him. She looked shell-shocked.

Another burst of sympathy flowered inside him, but he hardened his heart against it. 'From this minute, you are not to contact him. In person. By phone. Or by any other means. *Capisce?*'

'Oh, I understand all right,' she spat, eyes glittering up at him. 'But as far as I'm concerned, you can go to hell!'

His blood pressure soared.

Why didn't she just do as she was told?

It might sound arrogant, but people—particularly women—were usually all too eager to do what he asked of them. This woman was like a beacon of defiance, beaming her lack of co-operation like a lighthouse gone crazy.

Infuriated, he tightened his arms around her. 'Say that again,' he snarled.

Her eyes widened.

And then she licked her lips.

Dio, but she shouldn't have done that, Luca decided.

She had sealed her fate with the swipe of a pink tongue.

With a groan, he grasped her shoulders, pulled her towards him and fused his mouth with hers.

Her lips were soft. And sweet. She tasted like nectar. Or honey. A wave of lust rocked him, so hard and so fast he wanted nothing more than to pull up her skirt and take her right that very minute.

He cupped the back of her head, then ran his fingers over the thick swathe of her silky hair. The action set off a fresh wave of orange scent, making him decide that what he could smell was her shampoo.

He stroked a hand down her back, stopping at the base of her spine. And still he kept on kissing her.

And slowly, inch by inch, the stiffness melted out of her body and she began kissing him back.

The top of Luca's head almost exploded. She had a taste all of her own. A feel all of her own. She was like heaven in his arms.

Luca backed her towards the desk. Something fell to the floor with a loud crash but he didn't bother looking to see what it was. He wanted the kiss to go on and on, wanted the vision in his head—the one where she was naked except for the black leather I'm-in-charge boots—to become reality.

He urged Morgan onto her back without breaking the connection of their mouths. She didn't protest. Instead, she wound her arms around his neck and clung to him as if she never wanted to let him go.

It was then that he smelled it.

Cologne.

Expensive cologne…but cloying.

The kind Joseph always wore.

Luca jack-knifed straight and staggered backwards. The taste of her on his tongue changed from sweet to sour in the blink of an eye.

He wiped a hand across his mouth, bile rising up in the back of his throat as he stared at her.

Morgan had pushed herself up onto her elbows. She was breathing heavily. The top two buttons of her blouse were undone. Luca didn't remember undoing them but he must have. He had a glimpse of lilac lace and the creamy swell of her breast before she clutched the open sides together.

And suddenly the image of her lying naked except

for the boots was back. Only this time it wasn't his
body entwined with hers...it was Joseph's.

His stomach clamped down tight, a wave of nausea
clutching at the back of his throat.

He found the thought of Joseph and Morgan together
totally repugnant.

And not just because Joseph was married to his
sister...but because he wanted her himself!

His eyes snapped back to her face.

She looked so innocent.

And at the same time so sensual.

It was a seductive mixture.

So much so that he could almost forgive Joseph for
being tempted to stray from his marriage and into
Morgan's bed.

Almost.

But not quite.

Honour had to come before lust.

Just as duty had to come before pleasure.

Joseph had married Stefania; it was his duty to
honour those vows.

No matter how tempting the package.

And it was very, *very* tempting...

'Keep your hands off me!' she spat.

Luca rocked back on his heels, fury riding his spine
like a bucking bronco. 'Why? Are you afraid I'll tell
your lover about how you fell apart in my arms? Don't
you think Joseph would like that?'

Lover?

Luca thought Joseph was her *lover?*

Morgan scrambled off the desk and turned her back
on him. She was shaking so hard it took three attempts
to rebutton her blouse.

She didn't know what shocked her more. Kissing Luca da Silva as if she wanted to devour him or the fact that he'd just suggested... Well, what he'd just suggested.

She shook her head.

When Luca had challenged her about her relationship with Joseph, she'd assumed he'd discovered the secret that they were father and daughter. Instead, he thought they were lovers.

If the idea wasn't so ludicrous, she'd have laughed in his face.

Instead, she almost cried.

What was already a complicated situation had just got one hell of a lot more complicated.

'Nothing to say?' Luca prompted behind her.

Although she knew he was goading her, Morgan spun around to face him. 'Joseph is *not* my lover! How can you suggest such a thing? The idea is ridiculous!'

'Is it?'

She angled her chin into the air. 'Of course it is. The man is old enough to be my—' She broke off and swallowed. What she'd been about to say was too close to home to utter out loud. 'He's a lot older than me.'

'You aren't the first young woman to have an affair with a wealthy older man.'

She was so tempted to fling the truth at him she could taste the words on the tip of her tongue. But Morgan forced herself to swallow them back. She'd promised Joseph she wouldn't say anything. And, while she thought they were digging a deeper hole for themselves by keeping the details of his paternity a secret, she wasn't prepared to go against his wishes.

It might have been different if Joseph were feeling a hundred percent. But these chest pains were no laughing matter. The last thing he needed was for her to present him with another problem when he already had enough on his plate.

Besides, she owed him.

Joseph had given her so much in terms of love and support. Honouring his request to keep their relationship a secret didn't even begin to repay him for all that he'd done for her.

'Except I'm not having an affair with him!' she flung back at him. 'You can't throw around outrageous accusations like that without a shred of proof!'

His jaw squared. 'I have proof.'

Her insides stilled at the same time as her heart took off at a gallop. 'You do?' she choked out, barely able to squeeze the words out past numb lips.

'You were seen.' His voice was hard. 'Together.'

She blinked, swallowed, felt her stomach muscles cramp. Maybe she should have kept quiet and not challenged him. She had a bad habit of letting her mouth run away with her.

'Who saw us? When? Where?' she demanded, thinking attack was the better form of defence. 'I want a list of dates. Places.'

His mouth compressed into a thin line. 'I'd rather keep that information confidential.'

She slammed her hands on her hips. 'And I'd rather you tell me!'

His skin tightened across his bones until it looked as if each feature had been carved from the most unyielding granite. 'Let's just say it's someone who works here who has been suspicious about your relationship for some time.'

Morgan couldn't think of anyone she dealt with here

at Da Silva Chocolate who would say such a thing. All the people she worked with were friendly and professional. 'I see. So you're taking the word of one person over another? They could just be some kind of troublemaker.'

'It is not.'

She bit back a frustrated sigh, tension forcing her shoulders to lift towards her ears. 'Damn it. This isn't fair! You're not giving me a chance to defend myself.'

His head went back, as if he was offended by the remark. 'I'll say this much, I believe you're rather fond of a pub called The Minstrel.'

She nodded. 'The food is terrific. You should try it some time.'

His eyes narrowed. 'So you admit it?'

'I admit we've had lunch there together, but that doesn't mean we're having an affair.'

His hands clenched at his sides. 'You kissed him. He kissed you.'

Morgan was sure they had. 'I'm not surprised. We often greet each other with a hug and a kiss. We often say goodbye that way too.'

His face hardened. 'That isn't funny.'

'I'm not trying to be funny. How do you greet *your* female friends?' He didn't answer, but his expression told its own story. 'You see. You do it, too.'

'There are kisses…and there are kisses.'

'I agree,' she said with an emphatic nod, trying and failing not to think about the kiss *they'd* shared several minutes ago. On a heat scale of one to ten, she'd rate it as a twelve: blistering. 'So, did your *informant*—' She made it sound like a dirty word. '—fill you in on the details? Did we kiss on the cheek or on the lips? Were our mouths open or closed? There's a hell of a difference, you know. How long did it last for? Were—?'

He grabbed her before she had the chance to finish, his fingers tight around her shoulders, his face so close to hers she could almost taste the feel of his mouth on hers. 'I didn't ask for all the sordid details.'

She reached out to push him away, but somehow ended up holding onto him instead. 'Then you should have,' she said. 'I'm no lawyer, but surely what you've just described is nothing more than circumstantial evidence?'

His mouth curled. 'I'm sure it wouldn't take much digging to find enough evidence to bury you right up to your pretty little neck.'

'Don't do that!' The words were out before she could stop them. The last thing she wanted was for Luca to start investigating her. It wouldn't take long for a detective agency to uncover her relationship to Joseph.

He stared at her through narrowed eyes. 'Why not?'

She scrabbled around for a suitable reply. For a moment her mind remained frustratingly blank. And then the simple answer presented itself. 'Because you'd be wasting your time, that's why,' she said, angling her chin into the air. 'There's no way you can find proof of something that doesn't exist.'

The look on his face told her he didn't believe her.

She huffed out a sigh. 'I really don't know why you find it so difficult to believe Joseph and I are friends. With everything he's been going through he needs someone to talk to. Joseph has been very concerned about Stefania's mental state. Although she's been a real trouper about the IVF treatments, the failure of their latest attempt really shattered her. He doesn't think she can take any more.'

Luca froze. His eyes glazed with anger.

Morgan clapped a hand to her mouth. She'd done it again! Hadn't thought before she spoke, her mouth running off before her brain had a chance to catch up.

Luca's hands tightened on her shoulders. 'How do you know about my sister's infertility problems? Who told you about the failure of the IVF treatment?'

He was so angry, Morgan trembled, her heart pounding out fear in her chest. She opened her mouth. Closed it again. She'd dug herself a hole. Saying anything more would merely give him ammunition to bury her.

Besides, they both knew there was only one answer to those questions.

Luca must have simultaneously drawn the same conclusion. His nostrils flared, hands tightening on her shoulders. Then he thrust her away, such a look of disgust and contempt on his face that she shuddered.

'We both know the answer to that, don't we?' he bit out through clenched teeth. 'The only person who could have told you is Joseph himself.'

Morgan didn't deny it. She couldn't. There was no one else who *could* have told her. Stefania and Joseph had been treated in a private clinic that was paid very well to be discreet.

Luca's lips curled into a snarl. 'And you dare to look me in the eye and declare you aren't lovers. It wouldn't be my idea of pillow-talk, but that's obviously when you prised the information out of him.' He gave her a glacial stare. 'I don't know what turns my stomach more. The fact that he's sleeping with you or the fact that he's been so indiscreet.'

'I—'

He held up a hand and she snapped her mouth closed.

'If you so much as breathe one word of what you've learned to the press, I'll sue you for everything you own,' Luca slated, back in control again as he stalked around the desk and resumed his seat. 'And if you come within shouting distance of Joseph again, you'll regret the day you ever met me!'

'You haven't heard a word I've said, Luca,' Michaela complained, touching him on the arm to get his attention.

She was right. He hadn't. Not a single word.

His mind was elsewhere.

With Morgan Marshall.

He kept thinking back to their meeting. The more he thought about it, the more it bothered him.

The way Morgan had flung the cheque back in his face disturbed him. Somehow it just didn't fit with the kind of woman she was. She should have taken the money and run.

Only she hadn't.

And then there was the way she'd kept on defying him. That didn't make sense either.

She should have taken the opportunity to try and attract him, not argue with him. After all, he was far wealthier than Joseph would ever be—not to mention younger and better-looking.

But Morgan hadn't given a damn what he thought of her.

It was those apparent anomalies that were making it so damned difficult to put thoughts of her out of his head.

It had nothing to do with those wicked black I'm-in-charge leather boots. It had nothing to do with thickly lashed black eyes and slanting cheekbones. And it certainly had nothing to do with the seductive curve of her mouth or how she'd tasted when he kissed her.

'Luca!'

Luca blinked and frowned at the blonde sitting across from him. 'What?'

'I was talking to you.' Now that she had his attention, she was all smiles. 'As I was saying…'

Luca tuned her out again.

He'd had enough of Michaela. Her company had begun to pall.

Since when? a little voice asked inside his head.

He hadn't been the least dissatisfied when he'd made love to her the night before. He hadn't thought about ending things until—he dragged in a deep breath—someone he wanted more had crossed his path.

He stared across the table. Suddenly he saw Morgan Marshall sitting there, with her brightly defiant eyes and flyaway hair.

Irritation, annoyance and anger clamped his jaw tight.

Desire hardened everything else.

'Luca!'

Luca looked up blankly. Michaela was out. He wouldn't be sharing her body or her bed again. And he'd tell her exactly that when he—

The phone in his pocket vibrated. Out of respect for the other diners, he'd switched off the ring tone on both of the phones he'd brought with him.

Dipping his hand into his jacket pocket, he used his fingertips to sense which phone was receiving a call and pulled it out.

It was the slimline Nokia.

Joseph's phone.

It had been easy to convince his brother-in-law to

leave it behind. Mobile phones could be problematic in other countries. Some worked fine. Others didn't. Much easier, Luca had suggested, to use the local mobile phones he'd arranged to be ready and waiting for them on their arrival in Sydney.

Stefania had been equally persuasive. She didn't want Joseph working while they were away. They deserved a holiday. Why not leave the phone and let Luca handle all his business calls?

Luca hazarded a guess this wasn't a business call.

Not only was the number unregistered, but a glance at the platinum and gold watch adorning his wrist told him it was eight-forty, too late under normal circumstances for any of Joseph's business colleagues to be calling him.

'Excuse me,' he said to a pouting Michaela. 'I have to take this.'

He put the phone to his ear and pressed the button to connect the call. 'Hello?'

Silence greeted him.

He pulled the phone away from his ear and looked at the screen, checking to see if the caller had hung up. The display showed the call was still connected, its duration ticking over as he watched.

He put the phone back to his ear. 'Hello? Is anyone there?'

Still all he could hear was silence. No, he was wrong about that. If he listened carefully he could just make out the sound of someone breathing. 'Hello? Can you hear me?'

The back of his neck prickled. His fingers tightened around the phone and some instinct made him say, 'Morgan…?'

He heard a faint gasp, barely a whisper of sound, and then the line went dead.

Luca exhaled sharply as icy fury sliced through him. *Madre del Dio!*

The little witch had called her lover despite everything he'd said to her today.

His hands clenched into fists.

He'd let Stefania down once before; he wouldn't do so again.

It would take someone a hell of a lot smarter than Morgan Marshall to get the better of him.

In the end his will would prevail.

As it always prevailed.

It was time to up the ante.

Oh, yes, it was time Morgan learned just how serious he was about this.

He thrust back his chair and stood up, ignoring completely the fact that they hadn't finished their meal. 'We're leaving!'

CHAPTER THREE

MORGAN REACHED OVER and picked up the bright red cushion from the opposite end of the couch and put it behind her with its twin. Leaning back, she sighed.

She should be updating her résumé. Or trawling through employment websites for suitable vacancies.

But she couldn't stir up enough motivation to do either.

It wasn't that she was lazy; she just wasn't ready to accept that her job was gone for good.

She'd never been a quitter and she wasn't about to start now.

When she finally got hold of Joseph and told him what had happened he'd have her reinstated.

Or would he…?

She'd thought so…until the doubts had begun to creep in.

What if Joseph decided it was safer for her to get a job elsewhere? Considering how determined he was to keep her identity a secret, it was entirely plausible he'd support Luca's decision.

The realisation sent her heart plummeting towards her toes and her hand reaching for the panacea for all ills—chocolate.

Morgan bit down on her lower lip as she pondered her selection. It was between a caramel ganache and a praline infused with cinnamon—two of her favourites. Deciding to leave both for later, she chose a frangelica cream log instead.

Opening the black foil wrapper emblazoned with the tiny silver Da Silva logo, she popped the chocolate in her mouth then blissfully closed her eyes.

Delicious.

When the last piece of lusciousness melted away, she opened her eyes.

The first thing she saw was the notepad she'd been using to figure out her finances.

It was time to face reality again.

Sighing, she picked up the pad.

Her loan and mortgage repayments were at the top of the list. Then came other basic necessities: food, electricity, gas, and enough money to take the tube to and from job interviews. A lot of these latter figures had been crossed out—some more than once—as she'd tried to pare them back to the absolute minimum.

The bottom line made her gulp.

Although she had some savings—with no family to help her after her mother died she'd needed the security of having something to fall back on—they were nowhere near enough to cope with her outgoings.

She could rework the numbers until she used up all the ink in her pen, but the result would be the same.

Unless she found a job—soon—she was screwed.

Morgan flung the pad and pen back down on the coffee table.

Drat Luca da Silva!

This was all his fault.

She gritted her teeth.

She couldn't stop thinking about him.

It had nothing to do with black eyes flecked with gold or a face that would make any woman look twice.

And it certainly had nothing to do with how he'd kissed her. As if she belonged to him. As if she was the most desirable woman on earth.

No, his outrageous behaviour was the reason she was finding it impossible to get him out of her head.

Sighing, she picked up the box of chocolates again. Her fingers were hovering over a pyramid of dark, milk and white chocolate layers when the doorbell rang.

Uncrossing her legs, she put the chocolate box on the couch and pushed herself to her feet. Unbolting the door, she pulled it open.

She was so unprepared to find Luca da Silva standing on the doorstep that she stood staring up at him with her mouth open.

Tonight he was wearing a pair of tailored black pants and a cream ribbed sweater beneath a black leather coat. He looked dark and dangerous and far too handsome for his own good.

'Don't you know you should never open your door without checking who it is first?' he said with a frown. 'It could have been anybody.'

She clutched the neckline of her pale blue satin dressing gown together. 'It was. What are you doing here, Luca?'

'I would have thought that was obvious. I'm here to see you. Aren't you going to invite me in?'

Her spare hand gripped the edge of the door, barring his entry. 'No, I'm not going to invite you in. You're not welcome in my home.'

'You'd rather have our discussion out here in the hallway with your neighbours listening in?' he asked, cocking his head to the left, where old Mrs Addison's beady eyes could be seen glued to the door opening.

'Since I have no intention of talking to you there will be nothing to listen to.' She paused, her heart leaping into the back of her throat. 'Unless you've changed your mind about having me fired?'

'No. I haven't changed my mind.'

Her heart fell. 'Then we have nothing to discuss. Now, go away!'

She tried to push the door closed, but the tip of an expensive black leather shoe wedged itself in the doorway. 'Let me in, Morgan.'

She was about to demand that he leave immediately or she'd call the police, but then she hesitated. Antagonising Luca wasn't going to do her a damned bit of good. In fact, it could be counter-productive.

Where was the harm in listening to what he had to say? She might even be able to persuade him to get her her job back.

'I guess I can spare five minutes,' she said grudgingly. Pulling open the door, she held her arm out wide. 'Come in.'

Luca swept past her.

Her small lounge room looked even smaller with Luca in it. His height and the sheer energy he emanated seemed to shrink the room to half its normal size.

Luca looked around. When he saw the distinctive Da Silva packaging—rich, glossy black shell emblazoned with the silver embossed swirl of the Da Silva logo—he walked over and picked up the box.

'This is the latest line,' he said, inspecting the lid.

She shrugged. 'If I'm going to market a product I have to know everything about it. Including what it tastes like.'

'But you no longer work for Enigma Marketing. Remember?'

Her mouth compressed into a thin line. 'How can I forget? If you must know, they happened to be the only chocolates I had on hand.'

'And you're working your way through the entire box?' he asked, looking at the pile of scrunched-up wrappers on the coffee table.

She angled her chin into the air. 'So what if I am? I've had a bad day, thanks to you.'

'Hmm.' Luca ignored her comment as he inspected the contents of the box. 'Do you know you can tell a lot about a person by their choice of chocolate? Going by what you've demolished so far, I'd say that you are bold and adventurous.' He looked up, his eyes meeting hers. 'I'd also say that you're not averse to taking risks.'

'That's all very interesting, but why are you here?'

Selecting a chocolate, Luca put it in his mouth. 'You know why. It's about one of those risks I just mentioned.' His eyes narrowed to dark slits in a face carved from granite. 'How dare you call Joseph when I expressly ordered you not to?'

'Who said I called him?' she asked, stalling for time.

'I do. You called. I answered.' He raised a brow. 'Remember?'

She angled her chin into the air. 'I don't know what you're talking about.'

'Really? Why don't we test that theory?'

She frowned, and then paled when he fished a mobile phone out of his coat pocket. He stared at her, a glint of challenge in his eyes as he pressed a button.

'Don't,' she choked.

It was too late. The mobile phone sitting on her kitchen bench began ringing.

Luca pulled the phone away from his ear. 'Aren't you going to answer that?'

She shook her head and closed her eyes. 'No.' How was she to know that Joseph had left his phone with Luca? How was she to know that Luca would guess it was her calling? 'Oh, for goodness' sake—hang up, will you?'

Luca depressed the button and the apartment fell silent.

She angled her chin into the air. 'I'll call who I like. You can't tell me what to do.'

He stared back. 'Then you'll suffer the consequences.'

Slamming her hands on to her hips, she glared at him. 'Stop threatening me, Luca! It isn't going to work.'

She could tell by the look on his face that her answer had surprised him. He remained silent for a long time, eyes fixed on her face.

Morgan stared straight back.

Finally, he asked, 'Why did you call him, Morgan?'

'Why do you think? I wanted to tell him you'd had me fired!'

He crossed the room until he was standing right in front of her, so close she could smell wine on his breath. 'Why? Were you hoping he'd get you your job back?'

She nodded. 'I love my job. Working on the Da Silva Chocolate account is the opportunity of a lifetime. I know it. And so do you. I worked hard to get my position and I've worked hard to keep it. It's not fair that you're taking it away from me.'

'You should have thought of that before you started sleeping with Joseph!'

She flung her hands into the air, then quickly gathered the sides of her robe together when she realised the action had pulled the neckline apart. 'For heaven's sake! How many times do I have to tell you? I'm *not* sleeping with him. And even if I was it's not a justifiable reason for having me fired!'

'I'm making it a reason.'

Morgan gritted her teeth. 'You are so arrogant it makes me sick. I could lose my apartment. Have you thought about that? I have a mortgage. How am I meant to make the repayments without a job?'

Luca frowned, as if the thought had never occurred to him. 'I'm sure your family will be happy to help you out until you find something else.'

'Not everyone is as rich as you, Luca,' she said, deliberately avoiding making any direct comment about her family.

Joseph would loan her the money if she asked him. But she wouldn't ask. Not only would it be another thing he'd have to hide from his wife, but she didn't want Joseph to think she'd contacted him because of what she could get out of him financially.

She'd contacted him out of a sense of personal identity. She'd needed to know where she came from. Who she was. She and her mother had been so different. She'd often felt like a square peg in a round hole. Meeting Joseph had given her a sense of herself she'd never had before. They connected in a way she and her mother never had.

'I see.' He was silent for a long moment. 'I'd be willing to make you a loan.'

'I just bet you would. With strings attached, no doubt!'

He nodded. 'I'd give you a loan in exchange for your agreement to stay away from Joseph.'

She clamped her hands into fists. 'Forget it!'

A sense of danger permeated the air. She felt as if she was holding a tiger by the tail. Every time she defied Luca it was as if she was pulling on that tail. Strangely, the thought didn't frighten her. Instead, there was a tingle of something very akin to excitement rippling down her spine.

She could see by the glint in his eyes that Luca felt it too.

Suddenly the awareness was back, threaded like a spider's web between them.

Barely able to breathe, she licked her lips and whispered, 'No.'

Even before it happened she knew what was coming.

He tunnelled a hand under her hair and around her neck, then dropped his head and kissed her.

And she, God help her, kissed him right back.

Unlike the first time, she didn't even pretend to resist.

Somehow her arms found their way up around his neck, her fingers digging into his hair. He smelled warm and sensually male. She pushed her aching breasts against the hard wall of his chest.

Their bodies came together as if they'd been programmed to do so. Each hollow was met by a corresponding curve, until they fitted together like pieces of a jigsaw puzzle.

Softness met hardness.

Heated flesh met other heated flesh.

Luca groaned and pushed a thigh between her legs. Her body pulsed. Her blood thickened. Her breathing became non-existent.

She clutched at his shoulders, as much to hold herself upright as to feel the strength and power of him under her hands. In that moment it didn't matter who he was. Didn't matter that being in his arms meant she was playing with fire. All that mattered was the aching need he'd ignited inside her.

'Luca…'

Luca heard the breathless wonder and desperate need in Morgan's voice.

Instead of giving him pleasure, the realisation chilled him.

Did she say Joseph's name in that exact same tone as they made love? Did she shudder and hang on to Joseph the same way she was clinging to him?

Joseph again.

Ice filled his veins. He lifted his head. 'I wonder what Joseph would say if he could see you now.'

She flinched and shoved against his chest but Luca refused to let her go. 'Leave Joseph out of this!'

If only he could!

Life would be a lot less complicated if Morgan had never been involved with Joseph. They would probably already be lovers by now, Luca realised. He would have acted on the initial attraction and swept her off her feet.

'I will if you will,' he said, his heart suddenly beating strongly.

She tossed her head. 'Meaning…?'

'Forget about him.' He pressed his hips against her, letting her feel his arousal. 'If you need a lover, have me instead!'

Morgan gaped. Blinked. Shook her head. And all the while her heart was hammering away like a jack hammer in her chest.

'What did you say?' she gasped out.

He smiled. To Morgan's way of thinking it was a very predatory smile. 'You heard me. Forget about Joseph. If you want a lover, why not have me?'

That was what she'd thought she'd heard.

But she was sure she must have been mistaken.

One look at Luca's face assured her she wasn't. He was looking at her with an intense kind of hunger that immediately made her heart thrum even faster.

'I've been told that I'm good in bed,' he continued.

Morgan could believe it. If the way he kissed was anything to go by, then making love with Luca would blow her apart.

'I'm also generous to my mistresses,' Luca added.

He sounded as if he was reading a list of qualifications, Morgan thought with a tinge of hysteria.

'I'd be happy to give you a demonstration,' he murmured, his voice running like liquid chocolate down her spine.

Morgan exhaled sharply and pushed against his chest. 'No! Don't!'

Every time he kissed her, he weakened her defences. She had to remain strong. Even though there was a part of her that wanted to know what it would be like to make love to this man she knew she would be crazy to do so. Getting involved with Luca would be inviting disaster.

He was Joseph's brother-in-law; sleeping with him was out of the question.

'But I insist.'

'No…!'

'No?' He sounded surprised, as if he'd never been turned down before. 'Are you sure about that?'

'Of course I'm sure.' To show him just how sure she

was, she pulled out of his arms, stalked to the door and wrenched it open. 'Your five minutes are up. Please leave.'

He strolled towards her, hands in his pockets, looking handsome and sophisticated and completely unconcerned. 'Perhaps I didn't make myself clear.' His eyes drilled into hers. 'What I meant was that you either agree...or face the consequences.'

Morgan gasped and paled. 'There's nothing you can say or do to make me agree to be your mistress.'

He smiled. 'Do you really believe that?'

She nodded.

His smile widened. 'When I want something, I always get it.'

'Well, you're not getting me.'

'Oh, yes, I am.' The gleam in his eyes made the gold flecks stand out prominently. 'I just have to find your weakness. Your Achilles' heel.'

She tossed her head. 'I don't have one...unless you're talking about the heels on my feet.'

'No.' He met her gaze with a piercing look. 'I'm talking about...Joseph.'

He said Joseph's name as if it was a sword he was thrusting through her. She was so stunned she wasn't able to hide her reaction.

She flinched.

Luca watched her with almost clinical detachment. 'I thought that might get your attention.'

'What do you plan on...on doing to him?' she asked, barely able to force the words out past numb lips.

'I don't know. I'll have to think about it.' He gave her a narrow-eyed stare. 'For some strange reason my sister loves him. So I won't be able to do anything too dramatic. But I'll think of something.'

Morgan swallowed around a lump the size of a football in her throat. Panic seized her. She didn't know what to say—or do—as anxiety rushed at frantic speed around her body.

'Perhaps if you can't be relied on to stay away from him it's time I started putting pressure on Joseph. A threat here, a warning there. It could work wonders.'

Her tension wound tighter, drawing her shoulders up towards her ears. She tried to imagine the kinds of threats Luca could employ against Joseph, but she couldn't seem to string two thoughts together.

'He has a fondness for his job at Da Silva Chocolate. Perhaps it's time I replaced him.' His eyes remained fixed on her face. Steady. Determined. Unrelenting. 'Olivia is doing a good job. Maybe it's time I promoted her.'

Morgan gritted her teeth together, her eyes never leaving his face. Inside, she was trembling.

Was this how she was going to repay her father for unhesitatingly welcoming her into his life? By getting him fired?

Luca smiled, looking cool and relaxed. 'That may not be enough, though. I should imagine he's quite besotted with you. But I know what *would* work.' He reached out and stroked a finger down her cheek. 'Aren't you going to ask me what it is?

He was enjoying toying with her. Well, she was not going to play the mouse to his cat.

Angling her chin into the air, Morgan spat, 'I wouldn't give you the satisfaction!'

He laughed. 'I can't wait to find out if you have this much fire in bed.'

Morgan blushed to the roots of her hair. His comment was so unexpected. So was the sudden rush of heat that pulsed between her legs and tightened her nipples into tight beads of arousal.

'I'm feeling generous, so I'll tell you anyway. You see, what you may or may not realise is that Joseph loves Stefania. He might be temporarily captivated by you, but it won't last. All I'd have to do is threaten to tell Stefanie about you and he'd kick you out of his life so fast your head would spin.'

'I know he loves her. I'm not stupid. If it ever comes to a choice between Stefania and me Joseph will obviously choose his wife.'

And, for the umpteenth time in her life, she would be relegated to second place, Morgan realised with a sinking heart. She should be used to it by now. Her mother had always put her lovers ahead of her.

Even though he loved her, her father would no doubt do the same. Even though he wanted her in his life as much as she wanted to be in his, his marriage would be his first priority

'Only he'll never have to make that choice,' Morgan continued, angling her chin into the air. 'Because we're *not* having an affair! So you can stop threatening me.' She gave him a look down the length of her nose. 'Besides, we both know you won't say anything to Stefania. You wouldn't do anything to hurt her.'

He gave her a grim-faced smile. 'Want to bet?'

Her stomach began to churn, a cold sweat breaking out on her skin. 'You wouldn't!'

'No? In the long run it could be for the best. She can do without a cheating husband. Our mother had one affair after another. Stefania saw what that did to our father. She'd hate to get caught up in the same kind of relationship.'

God! He was telling her the truth.

She couldn't let Luca speak to Joseph—or Stefania.

Because Luca was right.

Joseph would drop her like a hot potato if she became a serious threat to his marriage. Worse, he would blame her for the break up and end up hating her. Worse still, the mere pressure of the confrontation and the choice he had to make could make those chest pains develop into something far more catastrophic.

She couldn't let that happen.

Wouldn't let that happen.

Joseph meant everything to her. He wasn't just her father. He was also her friend and mentor, always ready to listen and generous with his advice and support.

She would do anything to keep him safe. Would do anything to keep him in her life and retain that sense of belonging she'd always longed for.

But did *anything* include becoming Luca's mistress?

'Have you decided?'

Luca sounded so sure of himself.

So sure of *her.*

'No!' She curled her fingers into her palm. 'I can't decide right now. I need time to think.'

He shrugged. 'OK, think about it. You have until tomorrow morning to make your decision. And while you're at it think about this.'

Before she knew what he intended, he kissed her again.

Only their mouths touched.

But that was enough.

More than enough.

He kissed her as if he wanted to devour her.

He kissed her as if he wanted to absorb her soul.

Morgan was powerless against the onslaught. Much

as she knew she shouldn't, she leaned into him, her mouth softening as she kissed him back.

When they were both breathing heavily, Luca lifted his head and stared deep into her eyes. They stood like that for endless minutes. Then he placed a business card on the sideboard, turned and walked away, leaving Morgan standing on trembling legs staring after him.

As she watched him disappear down the corridor, anxiety filled her until she felt overflowing with it.

She was faced with a choice between two unsatisfactory options.

A dilemma of unprecedented proportions.

What the hell was she going to do?

CHAPTER FOUR

THE FOLLOWING MORNING Luca was in the middle of a meeting with his London executive team when his mobile phone rang.

'Excuse me,' he said to the faces directed towards him around the long boardroom table. He fished the phone out of his pocket and pressed the button to connect. 'Yes?'

'It's me.'

He recognised Morgan's husky voice instantly—how could he not when it played like a violin down his spine?—and realised she was calling him with her answer.

He'd been stunned yesterday to hear himself suggest he become Morgan's lover. He certainly hadn't planned on making the suggestion—he didn't need to advertise for bedroom partners. But as soon as the words had left his mouth he'd realised it was the perfect solution.

It would allow him to keep an eye on her and at the same time get her out of his system.

Leaning back in his chair, he ignored the surreptitious looks he was receiving from the executive team and kept his voice low. '*Buongiorno*, Morgan. How are you today?'

'You know how I am,' she snapped.

'Have you thought about what we talked about last night?' His gaze connected with Olivia's. She was staring at him with studied concentration, as if she were trying to read his lips or something. It wouldn't surprise him. She was an ambitious woman who was always on the look-out for opportunities to promote herself.

As soon as she saw him looking at her, she turned her attention to the man next to her and started a conversation.

'Yes, I've thought about it.' Her voice was so thin Luca could hardly hear her.

Anticipation held him still. 'And what have you decided?'

He heard her exhale. Then she said quietly but firmly, 'No. My answer is no. I won't be your mistress.'

'What…?' Luca roared, unable to contain himself as he jack-knifed straight.

His voice was so loud, and the action so violent, everyone in the room turned to look at him.

Luca ignored them.

'You heard me,' Morgan said. 'I won't be your mistress.'

Luca dragged in a breath, then threw his head back and laughed. His initial reaction had been one of shock; he wasn't used to anyone refusing him something he wanted. But now that he was over his initial surprise he felt a wave of excitement ride his spine.

He loved a challenge, and Morgan was proving to be a challenge in more ways than one. She was a beacon of defiance, resisting him at every turn.

It was a long time since a woman had done that. Usually all he had to do was crook his little finger to have whatever woman he wanted come running.

The thrill of the chase set his insides buzzing until it was all he could do to sit still.

He would win in the end, of course.

He always did.

But this time he had the feeling the journey would be half the fun.

'You're just dragging this out, you know,' he murmured. 'As I told you last night, I always get what I want.'

Morgan shivered.

Determination underlined each and every one of Luca's words. He was a force to be reckoned with in more ways than one. And the word 'no' obviously wasn't part of his vocabulary.

Turning Luca down had been difficult. She'd been torn in two entirely different directions until it had felt as though she were about to split in half.

But now that she'd made her decision she had to stick to it. She couldn't let Luca's over-blown confidence sway her. 'You can think that if you—'

'Hang on a moment.'

Morgan couldn't believe Luca had interrupted her mid-flow and was now talking to someone else. She was about to slam the phone down when part of the conversation she was unwittingly eavesdropping on stopped her.

Although she couldn't make out every word—Luca must have wrapped his hand around the phone—the words 'Stefania' and 'hysterical' came through clearly.

Her heart leapt into the back of her throat and the air locked tight in her lungs.

Joseph. My God! Had something happened to her father?

Barely able to hear Luca above the sound of her

blood pounding at her temples, Morgan forced herself to concentrate on what he was saying.

It soon became clear that he was now talking to his sister on another line. Although she could only hear bits and pieces, Luca was obviously urging Stefania to calm down. After a while he fell silent, as if were listening to her talk.

Finally Luca began speaking again. The words 'hospital' and 'Joseph' confirmed Morgan's worst fears.

The phone dropped from her nerveless fingers and clattered onto the coffee table. She scrambled to pick it up but she was shaking so hard it took three attempts. When she put the phone back to her ear she was greeted with silence. Dropping the phone must have accidentally disconnected the call.

She was about to redial—had actually pressed the call list button to do exactly that—when she had second thoughts.

If she sounded only half as upset as Stefania was purported to be it would no doubt reinforce Luca's opinion that she and Joseph were having an affair—in which case he would probably tell her as little as possible about Joseph's condition.

There had to be a way of finding out how her father was doing without contacting Luca. She just had to figure out what it was.

Flinging herself down on the couch, Morgan dragged in several deep breaths and felt her heartbeat slowly return to normal. Feeling calmer, she mined her memory banks.

During her first conversation with Luca he'd told her that Stefania and Joseph were on his private jet on their way to Sydney, Australia.

That was her starting point.

Now all she had to do was use the internet to make a list of the hospitals in Sydney and then call them.

Two hours later Morgan almost jumped out of her skin when she finally hit the jackpot.

'Yes, a Mr Joseph Langdon was admitted earlier this evening,' the switchboard operator told her. 'I'll put you through.'

Morgan had been so focussed on finding Joseph she hadn't given the time difference a thought. Not that it mattered. Hospitals operated twenty-four-seven and must be used to people calling at all times of the day and night.

'Emergency. Can I help you?'

Morgan almost fainted when she realised which department she'd been put through to. 'Yes. I'm calling to see how Mr Joseph Langdon is doing.'

'Your name, please?'

Morgan frowned. 'I don't want to be put through to anybody. I just want to know what his condition is.'

'I understand that, but I need to know if your name is on the list.'

A frisson of unease unfurled serpent-like down her spine. 'What list?'

'The hospital is under strict instructions to discuss Mr Langdon's condition only with immediate family,' the nurse replied.

Morgan swallowed.

She *was* immediate family.

Not that the other woman knew that.

Not that *anyone* knew that.

It was on the tip of her tongue to blurt out the truth but she swallowed the words back. This was a fragile situation. She had to tread carefully. The last thing she wanted was to make the situation worse.

If she gave her name and it wasn't on the list the nurse might mention it to Stefania. Under no circumstance could that be allowed to happen.

Equally, she couldn't expect the nurse to believe that she was Joseph's secret daughter just on her say-so. If she wasn't dismissed as a complete fruitcake or a trouble maker, her story would probably be reported to the family.

Again, she couldn't allow that to happen.

Anxiety clawed at her insides. She was rapidly running out of options.

'Look, I'm not on your list. I'm a friend of Joseph's. Please just tell me how he is,' she pleaded. 'I won't tell anyone.'

'I'm sorry. If you're a friend of Mr Langdon's then I suggest you contact his family for information on his condition.'

The line went dead.

Morgan's heart sank like a stone.

She slumped back against the couch and pressed shaking fingers to her forehead.

Joseph was in Emergency.

The hospital was only revealing information to his immediate family.

Neither of those things sounded encouraging—in fact just the opposite.

Her father could be dying for all she knew.

She realised something else.

Whether she liked it or not, Luca was her only link to her father!

Morgan was pacing her apartment like a caged animal, hoping against hope that there was something she'd overlooked, when the doorbell sounded. She crossed to the door and pulled it open.

It was Luca.

He was the last person she was expecting, and for a moment all she could do was stand and stare at him.

He really was the most handsome man, she acknowledged, her heart doing a massive leap in her chest. Today he was dressed in a black hand made suit. His black hair was swept back off his forehead with the same arrogance she encountered every time he opened his mouth. Every feature was perfect in an entirely natural way, as if it had been sculpted by one of the masters. And his eyes…

They were amazing. A deep, intense black flecked with dashes of gold.

'That's a habit you have to break,' Luca said, frowning down at her.

Morgan blinked up at him. 'What is?'

'Opening the door without checking who it is. That's the second time you've done it. It's dangerous.'

She knew he was right. 'OK. Next time I will.'

'Good. See that you do.' He looked past her into the apartment. 'Aren't you going to invite me in?'

She held the door open. 'Would it do me any good to refuse?'

'No.'

'What are you doing here, Luca?' she asked, closing the door and following him into the lounge room.

'What do you think I'm doing here?' He snagged her wrist and pulled her into his arms. 'I'm here to change your mind about becoming my mistress.'

'But—'

She never had a chance to finish. Luca kissed the words right out of her mouth.

From the moment his lips claimed hers she was lost. Heated pleasure swept through her in waves, almost knocking her off her feet. Light bloomed behind her closed eyelids.

She had one second of sanity when she managed to drag her mouth out from under his. 'Luca—'

Again, Luca didn't let her finish. He was every inch the predatory male as he backed her up against the front door, his mouth moving on hers as if he couldn't get enough of her.

Morgan could feel his heart racing in tandem with hers, could feel the press of his erection against her. His excitement triggered an answering response deep inside her, and what little sanity she had slipped away.

Luca lifted his head and stared deep into her eyes. 'Look me in the eye, *cara,* and tell me that you want me.'

She opened her mouth. Closed it again. Dragged in a breath and then another. 'I can't...'

'You can.' Luca pressed his hips closer to her. 'Feel what you do to me.'

Her body pulsed. 'I—'

He pressed a hard kiss on her mouth to silence her, then lifted his head. 'Say it.'

Confusion washed through her. What was she doing? This wasn't supposed to be happening.

She tore herself out of his arms and put some distance between them. 'I haven't changed my mind. I think it's time you left.'

'I don't think so. We didn't get a chance to finish our conversation earlier.' He sat down on the couch, making it clear that he wasn't about to leave. 'I apologise for the interruption. Did you stay on the line long?'

He'd tried to sound casual but didn't quite pull it off.

If it hadn't been for the look in his eyes—which Morgan would describe as watchful—she might have been fooled. He wanted to know how much she'd heard. Wanted to know if she knew Joseph was ill.

Gut instinct warned her to keep what she knew to herself. It might prove useful—although how she could use it to her advantage she wasn't quite sure.

She tossed her head. 'No, not long. I called you a few choice names, then slammed the phone down.'

He flashed her a smile. 'That sounds like you.'

'It does, doesn't it? Now, what are you doing here? You said we hadn't finished our conversation, but as far as I'm concerned we had. My answer was no, remember?'

'How could I forget? It's a long time since a woman has turned me down.'

'Going on the size of your ego, it sounds as though it's well overdue,' she fired back at him.

Luca threw his head back and laughed. 'I'm going to enjoy taming you.'

'You're not going to get the chance.'

'No?' Confidence oozed out of every pore.

She shook her head.

'Oh, I think I am.' He stared at her in silence for a moment before saying softly, 'I'm here to call your bluff.'

Her breath hitched in the back of her throat. 'What… what do you mean?'

'I think you said no to becoming my mistress because you doubt I'll go through with my threat of telling Joseph and Stefania about your affair. You're taking a gamble in much the same way a poker player does.' He looked her straight in the eye. 'As I said, I'm going to call your bluff.'

'Meaning?'

'Meaning that unless you agree, here and now, to

being my mistress I'm going to tell them.' He extracted
his mobile phone from his jacket pocket and held it up
in the air. 'Do I use this, or not?'

For a moment Morgan couldn't breathe. Then her
brain kicked into gear. Luca didn't really mean what he
said. He couldn't. It would be inhuman to confront
Stefania and Joseph while Joseph was sick in the
hospital. He might be hard, but he wouldn't be that
cruel—at least not to his sister.

But that was the point, wasn't it? She wasn't
supposed to know about Joseph's illness, was she?

Luca was no doubt counting on that—that was why
he'd been so interested in how much she'd overheard.

He was doing exactly what he said. He was calling
her bluff, hoping she'd fold without putting his claim
to the test.

He was clever.

Devious...but clever.

She couldn't help but admire his determination, even
though it infuriated her.

She looked away from him.

Her eyes landed on the oversized mug sitting in pride
of place on the sideboard. It was bright yellow, with
equally bright red lettering on the side which read 'Get
Well Soon.'

Joseph had presented it to her, along with a big con-
tainer of chicken noodle soup he'd bought at a local
Chinese restaurant, when she'd gone down with a heavy
dose of the flu soon after she'd come into his life.

The poor man hadn't been able to understand why
she'd burst into tears the minute he'd explained why
he'd shown up unannounced on her doorstep. But the
simple truth was that the caring gesture had meant more

to her than he could ever know. Her mother had always treated her childhood illnesses as a hassle that *she,* Sheila, had to endure rather than her daughter. She'd whinged to such an extent that Morgan had soon learned to pretend she was feeling well even when she wasn't.

The memory of Joseph's kindness that day made tears sting the backs of her eyes. He'd made her feel more welcome and more loved in the short time she'd known him than she had in the entire time she was growing up.

Last night, when Luca had given her his ultimatum, the scales had been balanced between two equally unsatisfactory options.

Her father's illness changed everything.

Now one option clearly outweighed the other.

If Luca was her only link to her father then she had no choice.

But he wasn't going to have it all his own way.

'OK, Luca. You win. I'll be your mistress.' She paused and dragged in a breath. 'But only if you agree to my conditions.'

His frown deepened. 'What conditions? You're hardly in a position to demand anything.'

She ignored the last bit. 'Condition number one, we have equal rights within this relationship. How it will be conducted is up to both of us to decide. You *don't* get to order me around.'

For a good minute Luca just stared at her through narrowed eyes. Then he sighed. 'I suppose that's fair enough. Stefania is forever telling me how bossy I am. But it goes with the territory. I wouldn't be where I am today if I was scared of making decisions or telling people what I want. So don't expect me to change overnight.'

'I won't. But you will try?'

He nodded. 'As long as it's within reason. You'll just have to remind me whenever I get too overbearing.'

'I will. You don't have to worry about that!'

Luca grinned. 'I didn't think I would. I've already noticed you're not afraid of saying what's on your mind.'

She cocked her head to one side. 'Is that a compliment or a criticism?'

'What do you think?' he countered.

'It has to be a compliment. You're not exactly shy about coming forward yourself!'

Luca inclined his head, then raised an eyebrow. 'Just how many of these conditions do you have?'

Morgan swallowed and squeezed her hands together. 'Just two.'

'Two?' he repeated. 'What's the other one?'

The tips of her ears began to burn. The nature of the remaining condition was something she wasn't quite sure how to put into words.

'The thing is—' Her eyes found his, then nose-dived away. Her fingers fiddled with the long gold chain hanging around her neck. 'The thing is…Well, the thing is I don't want to sleep with you just yet.'

Luca stared at her and kept on staring.

Then he threw his head back and laughed.

'That is—' He was laughing so hard he had to stop speaking for a full minute. 'That is the funniest thing I've heard in years.'

'It's not funny,' she said stiffly. 'I'm dead serious.'

The gravity in her voice wiped the smile from his face and made him jump to his feet. 'You can't be. The whole idea of becoming my mistress is so that we can sleep together.'

She blinked big dark eyes at him. 'I know, but… but…'

She reminded Luca of a deer he'd caught in his head-lights once. It had given him that same wide-eyed, fright-ened stare just before it had taken off into the forest.

'But what?'

'But I just can't do it.' She was really pulling on the chain now, so hard he thought it might break. 'Not just like…like that. We barely know each other.'

Luca couldn't believe his ears. Couldn't believe she was serious. 'We know we want each other. Or are you going to pretend you *don't* go up in flames every time I touch you?'

Her eyes slid away from his but just as quickly returned. 'No. I'm not going to pretend.' She took a deep breath. 'I…I do want you.'

His breath hitched. He captured one of her hands and curled his fingers around it. '*Dio,* Morgan. Did you have to say that?'

'Would you rather I had lied?' Her free hand contin-ued to twist the gold bauble between her breasts. Luca didn't even think she knew she was doing it.

'Hell, no! Hearing you say you want me turns me on like you wouldn't believe. But saying you won't sleep with me at the same time is a sure way to twist a guy into knots.'

She didn't say anything to that.

Because there was nothing to say?

Or because this was a carefully thought out strategy?

Give with one hand…take with the other.

His mother had been an expert at that particular tactic.

She'd used precisely that method to keep her marriage together despite her constant affairs. And she'd used the same technique with her children—vacillating between being the attentive and loving mother to the party girl totally uninterested in her offspring.

Was Morgan trying to manipulate him in much the same fashion?

His eyes narrowed. 'Just what sort of game are you playing? You've agreed to be my mistress. Now you're trying to renege?'

'I'm not trying to renege. I'm just asking for a bit of time. I hardly know you. I can't just go to bed with a perfect stranger. I just can't. Don't you understand?'

She was yanking on the chain so strongly now that Luca could see the metal digging into her neck. He wanted to reach out and stop her, but something held him back.

'I'm not as experienced as the socialites that you usually keep as your playthings. I need some time to adjust. To get to know you a little before we...before we...' Her face flamed. 'Before we take the next step.'

Luca stared at her. She wasn't faking her reaction; he'd bet money on it. She might be a good actress but she wasn't *that* good. He'd seen performances on the stage that were far less convincing.

Which meant what, exactly?

That she was shy? Nervous?

Both of those things implied that she was inexperienced, and that was something he knew she was not. The fact that she'd persuaded Joseph into her bed, thus betraying the wife he adored, proved she was seasoned in the art of making love.

Tension knotted his shoulder muscles until they were physically painful. His free hand raked through his hair and around the back of his neck, his eyes never leaving her face.

Her bottom lip trembled.

He remembered seeing his mother do the exact same thing.

And he remembered what she'd done next.

His jaw clamped tight as the memory washed over him.

His father had been pacing the entrance hall, waiting for his mother to come home. He'd often done that when she was having one of her affairs. Unbeknownst to him, Luca had often watched him from the top of the staircase.

When Margherita had finally arrived they'd argued, during which his mother had done what she so often had. Realising she was losing the argument, her face had crumpled, bottom lip trembling in just the way Morgan's was doing now. Luca's father had immediately stopped what he was saying and taken his distressed wife into his arms, little realising that she was smiling over his shoulder.

Luca remembered that smile.

Remembered the cunning, manipulative gleam in her eyes.

That day he'd promised himself he'd never be the sucker his father had been.

He would not let Morgan take advantage of him!

'I'm not used to waiting for what I want.' With renewed determination Luca swept an arm around her waist and pulled her close. The hand clenching the bauble was caught between their two bodies and the chain finally gave out, collapsing like a strand of over-cooked spaghetti between them.

'Oh!' Morgan looked down, clearly surprised. In doing so, she revealed the curve of her neck.

'*Dio!*' Luca lifted a hand to the red welt around her throat. 'You've hurt yourself.'

Morgan lifted a hand and winced as she touched the tender flesh.

Luca released her waist, but kept hold of her hand. 'Do you have a first-aid kit?'

'Yes. In the bathroom.'

Following her pointing finger, Luca led her down a short corridor to a brightly tiled bathroom. Opening the cabinet she indicated, he located the first-aid kit. Flipping open the lid, he riffled through the contents until he found a tube of antiseptic cream.

'Hold your hair up,' he instructed.

Morgan dutifully gathered the thick swathe of her hair between her hands and held it above her bent head. Luca watched her breasts lift in the mirror, then dropped his eyes to the back of her neck and frowned at the swollen red skin.

Twisting the top off the tube, he squeezed a small portion of cream onto his fingertip. 'This might hurt.'

She nodded.

He heard the hiss of her breath as he gently applied the cream along the length of the wound. 'That was a stupid thing to do,' he remarked grimly.

She shrugged. 'I didn't realise I was doing it,' she mumbled, confirming exactly what he'd thought at the time.

Which rather exploded his idea of manipulation, didn't it?

It was also an indictment on him. He'd put her in such a stressful position she'd been unaware of damaging herself.

Screwing the cap back on, he tossed the tube onto the marble vanity unit and stared at their twin reflections in the mirror. 'What if I say no?' he asked quietly.

Her head shot up, her hands dropping her hair, which fell around her shoulders like black silk. Their eyes met in the mirror. 'Then the deal is off!'

Luca knew Morgan possessed many talents, but he decided bluffing wasn't one of them. He could see the resolution in her eyes. Could see the resolve squaring her shoulders.

Sighing heavily, he asked, 'How long do you want?'

'One month,' Morgan answered, squeezing the words out through numb lips.

She didn't know what surprised her more. The tender way Luca had attended to her neck or the fact that he was prepared to negotiate a reprieve with her.

'One month?' Luca repeated incredulously. He shook his head. 'That's too long. What about forty-eight hours?'

Morgan's heart sank. She frowned and unlinked the fingers she'd automatically crossed behind her back. 'No. The whole idea is for me to get to know you better. I can't do that in two days.'

'I'm not waiting a month.'

The stubborn tilt of Luca's jaw told her she'd be wasting her breath trying to convince him to wait for that length of time. She'd known it was a long shot, but it had been worth a try. 'Two weeks. How about two weeks?'

A long minute passed while Luca just stared at her. Then he cupped the side of her face and rubbed her bottom lip with his thumb. 'Forget it!'

'A week,' she gasped out. 'How about a week?'

Luca took his time answering. Finally he sighed and nodded. 'OK. Agreed.'

'Good,' Morgan said briskly. 'I would suggest—'

She broke off as Luca swept an arm around her waist and pulled her in close. She pressed her hands against his chest and leaned back as far she could, away from the heat and the potent male smell of him.

'What do you think you're doing?'

'Sealing our arrangement.' Luca smiled a slow, sexy smile that made her heart somersault in her chest and liquid heat pool in her belly. 'What better way to do that than with a kiss?'

'But—'

'But what? If you're suggesting we do nothing more than hold hands for the next week, then you're out of your mind. I'm a man, not a boy. If you want to get to know me, then you can start getting to know me on a physical level, too.'

Her heart beat even harder, slamming against her ribcage as if it was trying to break free. 'What…what exactly does that mean?'

'It means that I intend to kiss you whenever I feel like it.' His mouth curved in another of those slow, sensual smiles, and this time it was her knees that threatened to buckle. 'And touch you whenever I feel like it.'

CHAPTER FIVE

MORGAN SWALLOWED AS Luca's head descended.

His lips brushed hers and then retreated.

She tensed and told herself not to react.

His lips brushed hers again—only this time they didn't retreat. This time they lingered, teasing her lips apart, tasting the tender flesh with his tongue.

It was a kiss unlike any other kiss they'd shared. Instead of demanding a response this kiss was a temptation, an invitation she could either reject…or accept.

Heat rushed through her, from the top of her head to the tips of her toes. Morgan braced her feet against the carpet, hoping it would help her resist the insidious creep of desire flowing through her blood stream.

She knew exactly what she should do.

Step back.

Break the connection.

Smile as if nothing had happened.

Instead, she groaned in the back of her throat, dug her hands into the hair on either side of his head and deepened the kiss.

Luca gathered her closer. So close it was as if their bodies were fighting to occupy the same space. The smell of him was all around her, invading her senses, making them spin out of control.

It was only when she felt his hand cup her breast that Morgan realised just what she was inviting. She'd never intended the situation to get out of control so quickly.

But then, she hadn't really been thinking at all, had she?

Grabbing his tightly corded forearms, Morgan drew back. 'Let me go, Luca!'

Luca lifted his head and searched her face. *'Dio!* How can you say no to that?'

Morgan swallowed and looked away from him. He had no idea just how close she'd been to giving in. She cleared her throat. 'I'd like to go to the zoo.'

Luca blinked. 'I beg your pardon?'

'I'd like to go to the zoo. For our first date.'

'First date?'

She nodded. 'Yes. Isn't that what we agreed? Or did you think one kiss was enough for me to change my mind about sleeping with you straight away?'

The guilty look on his face should have made her angry. Instead, she laughed. His expression reminded her of a little boy with his hand literally caught in the cookie jar. In that instant he was so far removed from the man who'd tried to bribe and threaten her that it was easy to forget any of it had taken place.

'Forget it, Luca. It isn't going to happen. Now, do you agree?' Seeing the blank look on his face, she said, 'We'll go to the zoo?'

He grimaced. 'If you insist.'

Morgan had given the location of their first date careful thought. Number one priority was to go somewhere public. She wanted to avoid an intimate dinner for two. 'I do.'

'Are you ready to go?'

Her eyebrow arched. 'Now…?'

'There's no time like the present.' His black eyes filled with sensual promise. 'The sooner the week starts, the sooner it will be over and I'll get what I want.'

She swallowed when she realised he meant her. 'I guess it will. I'll just get my—'

She broke off as a phone started ringing.

'I'm sorry,' Luca said, fishing his mobile out of his jacket. 'I forgot to switch it off.'

'That's OK.'

Luca looked at the screen, then at her, his expression alerting her as to who it was. 'I have to take this.'

'That's OK. I'll just get my things.'

Going into her bedroom, Morgan pushed the door until it was almost closed. What she was about to do was wrong. But surely the situation justified it?

Heart slamming against her ribcage, she put her ear to the crack and listened.

Luca waited until the door had closed behind Morgan before speaking. '*Ciao,* Stefania. I didn't expect to hear from you so soon. How is he?'

Stefania didn't return his greeting, instead getting straight to the point. 'The doctor…the doctor said Joe has had a heart attack.' She could barely get the words out through her tears.

'Are you sure it was a heart attack?'

'Of course I am sure,' she said shrilly, her accent thickening. 'The doctor has run several tests. They have confirmed my worst fears.'

'Do they know what caused it?'

'They suspect it is stress-related. Apparently he

has high blood pressure.' She broke into another bout of sobbing.

'Calm down, Stefania. You're going to make yourself ill.' He waited while she got herself under control. He could hear her breathing deeply before noisily blowing her nose.

'I'm scared, Luca. I'm scared he's going to die,' she whispered.

'He's not going to die,' Luca said firmly.

'If he does it will be my fault,' she sobbed. 'The IVF treatments have been harrowing. I've been so focussed on myself I haven't noticed the toll it's taken on Joe.'

'He is *not* going to die,' Luca reiterated. And if he did his sister wouldn't be the one to blame. No doubt trying to keep his affair with Morgan a secret from his wife was at least partly responsible. 'High blood pressure can be treated with medication. Once they have it under control, he'll be out of danger.'

'That's what the doctor said,' Stefania said, hiccupping over the last word.

'There, you see,' Luca said soothingly. 'He'll be back on his feet before you know it.'

'But what if there is permanent damage to his heart?' she wailed.

'Does the doctor think there's a chance of that?' he asked.

'He says no.'

'Well, he's the expert.'

'But what if he's wrong?' she asked, sounding as if she was going to burst into tears again at any moment.

His heart wrenched. It was frustrating being on the other side of the world. Words of comfort spoken down a telephone line weren't half as reassuring as actually being there. But he'd already asked Stefania if she wanted him to fly to Australia and she'd said no.

There had to be something he could do to ease her concerns. 'Would you like to get a second opinion? I'll call in the best cardiologist in Australia if that's what you want.'

'Oh, would you? I'd feel so much better,' she said, unable to hide her relief.

'Consider it done.'

'Oh, Luca! You spoil me rotten. So does Joe. How I managed to be so lucky to have both a husband and a brother who treat me the way you guys do, I'll never know.'

'You deserve it,' Luca said feelingly. After everything she'd been through—was still going through—she'd earned the right to be treated like a princess.

'I'm sorry for making such a fuss,' Stefania said, sounding a lot calmer.

'Don't be. You're worried about your husband. That's completely understandable.'

'I have another favour to ask you,' she said.

'What's that?'

'I'm worried about Baci. You know she doesn't like it when Joe and I go away. This thing with Joe…' She paused for a moment. 'I can't help thinking something might have happened to her.'

Baci was the cat Luca had bought for her when they'd first moved to London, not long after their parents had died. Stefania had been having a difficult time adjusting to their new life. Luca had given her the kitten in an attempt to distract her. It had worked. Given something else to focus on—and worry about—she'd soon settled in.

'You've got that wretched cat staying in the equivalent of the Hilton,' Luca said with a smile, trying to lighten her mood. He nodded to Morgan as she re-entered the room. 'I doubt she'll be pining away. In fact probably just the opposite. After living in the lap of luxury, it's highly likely she'll be big and fat by the time you get home.'

'Luca!' she wailed, half-serious, half-not.

'Don't worry,' he soothed. 'I'll check on her.'

He ended the call with another instruction for her to call him if there was any news, phrasing it carefully so Morgan wouldn't guess what he was talking about.

He slid the phone back into his pocket. 'Are you ready to go?'

As they stepped into the hallway, Morgan felt as if her head would never stop spinning. Everything—Joseph's illness and her agreement to become Luca's mistress—had happened so fast she was still trying to come to terms with it.

But if she'd had any doubts that she'd made the right choice, then listening in on Luca's conversation with Stefania had erased them.

Her decision had already paid off.

She now knew Joseph was suffering from high blood pressure and had had a heart attack. She had also learned the prognosis was good, although a second opinion was being sought.

Luca handed her into the same big dark car that had collected her the previous day.

Gino was behind the wheel.

'Good afternoon, Gino,' Morgan said.

His head turned so that his eyes met hers in the rear vision mirror. 'Good afternoon, Ms Marshall,' he said, putting the car in gear and pulling smoothly into traffic.

Her jaw dropped halfway to the ground when she

realised he'd spoken in almost perfect English, burred only slightly with an Italian accent.

'You speak English,' she accused the back of his head.

'Yes,' he said, nodding.

Heat rushed into her cheeks as she remembered what she'd said about him the previous day. 'Gino…'

He glanced in the mirror. 'Yes, Ms Marshall?'

'What I said yesterday…I'm sorry. I didn't mean it,' she said awkwardly.

He shrugged. 'Don't worry about it. I've been called worse.'

'Still, I shouldn't have said it.'

'Forget it. I have.'

She turned and found Luca staring at her with an odd expression on his face. 'What?' she asked.

He was studying her hard, as if she were a particularly interesting insect. 'Most people treat Gino as if he's invisible.'

She folded her hands in her lap. 'Then they're not very polite.'

As they drove through the busy London streets Morgan was very aware of Luca sitting beside her. The clean male smell of him mixed with the fragrant aroma of the leather seats. Every time they turned a corner his thigh brushed hers and a shot of electricity fired through her system. By the time Gino pulled into the zoo car park, she could hardly wait to get out.

Several hours later, Morgan tugged on Luca's shirt-sleeve. 'Come on, Luca. You can't stand here watching Spike all day.'

Spike was the leader of the pack of lions at London Zoo. Luca had taken one look and had been captivated.

They'd been watching the big cats' antics for well over an hour now.

Well, if she were honest, Luca had been watching the lions and *she* had been watching *him*.

Staring at his profile.

Watching the flash of his smile when Spike did something he liked.

For the last five minutes, however, she'd been looking backwards and forwards between them. It had been a sobering moment when she'd realised just how much they had in common.

Strength.

Pride.

And a steely determination to protect their own.

Much to her shame, Morgan realised that not once—until now—had she looked at their situation from Luca's point of view. She'd been so concerned about her own position—and Joseph's—that she hadn't given a thought to how their relationship must look to Luca.

It was public knowledge that Luca and his sister were close. And Joseph had told her just how protective Luca was of Stefania—to the point of being over-protective. She'd also heard it for herself when she'd listened to Luca's end of his telephone conversation with Stefania.

Luca thought she was some husband-stealing trollop trying to break up his sister's marriage. Of course he was going to do something about it; he wasn't the kind of man to sit back and do nothing.

And when it came right down to it, she'd have thought less of him if he'd ignored the situation.

But it was *the way* he'd chosen to defend Stefania that bothered her.

Coming after her the way he had was wrong.

Forcing her to be his mistress was wrong.

'I can't believe you've never been to London Zoo,' she said, pushing her thoughts aside.

'Well, I haven't. I never had the time. Stefania and I moved to London when I was eighteen. I was too busy studying and working and looking after her.'

'You moved here when you were eighteen?'

He nodded. 'Not long after our parents died.'

'I'm sorry.' She put a hand on his arm. 'I didn't realise you were so young when it happened.'

Luca stiffened and slowly turned in her direction. 'When what happened?'

Morgan swallowed at the cold look in his eyes. Once again she'd spoken without thinking first. She shrugged and tried to smile. 'Nothing. Come on, let's move on.'

She let go of his arm and turned away, but he snagged her wrist and spun her back around to face him. 'When *what* happened?' he asked through gritted teeth.

Morgan sighed. One of these days she'd think first and speak second. 'When the accident happened,' she said calmly, suppressing a sigh.

Luca dropped her arm as if touching her somehow contaminated him. 'And just who told you about that? Or need I ask?' His mouth curled. 'Joseph has some pretty strange ideas about what passes for pillow talk.'

Morgan didn't credit him with an answer. She just turned and stomped away, not caring whether he followed her or not.

'Where do you think you're going?' Luca demanded, two seconds before his hand landed on her shoulder and pulled her to a halt.

Morgan threw him a scathing look as she tried to shrug away from his touch. 'Anywhere. As long as it's away from you. If you think for one minute that I'm going to hang around and let you treat me like this then you have another thing coming. That remark was completely unnecessary!'

Luca stared at her for what felt like ages without saying a single word. Morgan stared straight back, her chin at a challenging angle.

Finally he said quietly, 'You're right. It was. I'm sorry.'

Luca heard the words emerge from his mouth and couldn't believe he'd actually said them.

What was wrong with him?

He had nothing to apologise for.

Nothing.

Anger climbed the rungs of his spine.

Joseph had discussed the accident—the most traumatic experience of Luca's life—with Morgan.

His teeth were gritted so tightly together he thought they might shatter. His hands clenched into fists, which he shoved deep into his pockets.

Dio! What was going on here?

Why on earth had he agreed to wait a week to sleep with a woman who'd seduced a married man into her bed? A woman he was meant to be punishing? A woman who didn't deserve his respect?

He raked a hand through his hair and suddenly realised Morgan was no longer standing beside him. He spun on his heel, only to see her rigid back walking in the other direction.

He stomped after her, clamping a hand on her shoulder and bringing her to a halt again. 'Where do you think you're going?' he demanded, for the second time in as many minutes.

'Anywhere. As long as it's away from you,' Morgan replied, repeating her answer and the scathing look that accompanied it.

A feeling of *déjà vu* flowed over him. They'd already had this conversation. This time, however, he wanted it to end differently. 'Why?'

She stabbed him in the middle of the chest with one pointed finger. 'Because you're not sorry at all. You apologised just now, but you didn't mean a word of it.'

Luca opened his mouth to deny the charge, but just as quickly closed it again.

'You see?' She jabbed him again, as if she wanted to drill a hole through to the other side. 'You can't even deny it.'

The pent-up anger inside him suddenly spewed forth. He pulled her onto her toes and put his face close to hers. 'Damned right I can't deny it. It turns my stomach to think of you sleeping with Joseph.'

Instead of drawing back, Morgan put her face even closer to his. Luca could smell the subtle scent of her orange shampoo invade his nostrils, could feel her breath, warm and soft, feather his face. 'I have *never* slept with Joseph. How many times do I have to tell you that? We're friends. That's all. What's it going to take to get it through that thick skull of yours?'

She didn't give him a chance to answer, yanking out of his grasp and marching away from him, back rigid, shoulders squared, head tilted with angry pride.

Luca followed more slowly.

What if she was right?

For the first time he seriously considered that question. When Olivia had told him of her suspicions, Luca had been quick to believe her. Olivia was an astute businesswoman. Perceptive. Ambitious. She'd worked in a number of his organisations over the last three years and during that time she'd proved that he could rely on her. And that he could trust her. Nothing she'd said or done since suggested that had changed.

Now he went back over their conversation. At the time, it had never occurred to him that she might be lying, but now he realised he had to give it serious thought.

Olivia had told him about her suspicions *after* she'd outlined her plan to bring the marketing of Da Silva Chocolate back in-house, for her to manage, and only *after* he'd told her he'd think about it.

His reaction to her proposal had been lukewarm at best.

Had Olivia realised that? Had she twisted a couple of innocent lunches into something they were not? Had she invented her suspicions in the hope it would tip his decision in her favour?

Ice slid down his spine, taking his heart with it.

He stared at the proud tilt of Morgan's head. She'd had that exact same look about her when she'd tossed his cheque back in his face

Her action had bothered him then.

It bothered him even more now.

It was a lot of money for anyone to turn down—particularly someone struggling to pay off a mortgage. And yet Morgan had done exactly that without blinking an eye. 'I don't care how much it is. I don't want it,' she'd said.

She'd refused to be bribed.

She'd refused to be threatened.

Surely that showed a person with integrity?

Surely that showed a woman who wouldn't stoop to sleeping with a married man?

He remembered the way Morgan's boss had sung her

praises. At the time he'd wondered whether they were talking about two different women.

Luca ground his teeth together, frustration drawing his shoulders up towards his ears.

Dio, but this was impossible.

A part of him wanted to believe Morgan was telling the truth.

But there was too much evidence against her.

The feeling she'd been lying during that first meeting.

The feeling she was hiding something.

They were both strong feelings. Strong enough, Luca was sure, to be believed.

Even if he discounted those intimate lunches for two that Morgan had admitted to, what about the fact that she knew about the IVF treatments Joseph and Stefania were going through? He knew for certain even their closest friends—friends who'd known them for decades—didn't know about those.

And yet Morgan did.

And if that wasn't enough to convince him then the very fact she'd agreed to be his mistress did!

His shoulder muscles knotted.

His stomach clamped into a tight ball.

She was playing with his head. Making up seem down. Left seem right.

It was time he put a stop to this once and for all!

Morgan was striding past the monkey enclosure, oblivious to their cheeky antics, when Luca caught up with her.

Once again he stopped her with a hand on her shoulder.

Still fuming, Morgan spun around to face him. 'What do you want, Luca? If you intend insulting me again, I should warn you that I'm not in the mood!'

'Is it insulting to tell the truth?' he fired back.

The breath whooshed from her lungs. 'You wouldn't know the truth if it got up and bit you on the backside!'

'Is that a fact?' he gritted.

'It certainly is. I'm telling you the truth, damn it! You're just not listening to me.'

They were like boxers facing off in a ring.

Morgan glared at Luca.

Luca glared straight back.

'Maybe I'd be more willing to listen to you if you hadn't agreed to be my mistress,' Luca said, his voice as effective as steel cutting through paper.

Her heart did a stutter step in her chest. 'What do you mean by that?'

'Well, it's obvious, isn't it? You only agreed to become my mistress because you didn't want me to tell Joseph and Stefania about your affair. That makes you as guilty as hell as far as I'm concerned!'

Her insides contracted on a wave of anxiety that sent a cold chill running through her body and shrank her skin over her bones.

She'd been so caught up with Joseph's illness she hadn't given a thought to how giving in to his blackmail must look to Luca.

But he was right.

It made her look as guilty as hell!

No wonder Luca kept throwing accusations around like confetti.

She couldn't tell him that Joseph's illness had prompted her to change her mind. If Luca realised she was using him to keep tabs on her father's progress he would cut off her information completely.

Unless she gave him some other explanation then her agreement looked like an admission of guilt.

But what did she say to convince him otherwise?

She scrabbled around for a suitable explanation but her mind remained frustratingly blank. She tried to invent something, but couldn't think of anything he wouldn't be able to shoot holes through in two seconds' flat.

And then it came to her.

It was a stretch, but there was just enough truth in it to make it believable.

At least she hoped so.

She squared her shoulders and stared him straight in the eye. 'Well, I'm not guilty! I obviously didn't explain myself properly.' She dragged in a breath and clasped her hands together in front of her. 'My mother died a few years ago from an overdose of sleeping pills and anti-anxiety medication,' she said quietly.

Luca's expression altered, his eyes softening with sympathy. 'I'm sorry. But what does that have to do with our current situation?'

'I'm getting to that.' She took her time. Her mother's death had come as a complete shock and was still difficult to talk about. 'If you tell Stefania that Joseph and I are having an affair—even though we're not—what effect do you think it will have on her?'

'My sister is *not* suicidal!' Luca denied hotly.

'Neither was my mother!' Morgan shot back at him. 'The coroner ruled that it was an accidental overdose. Can I take it Stefania is on anti-depressants?' she asked.

Luca shook his head. The expression on his face warned her that he didn't like where this was leading one little bit. 'No, she isn't. She's determined to fight it herself. And besides, she's not the type to overdose—accidentally or otherwise!'

'I could have said the same thing about my mother, and look how she ended up. OK, so Stefania's not on medication. But do you want to take the chance on her getting worse?' She didn't wait for him to answer. 'I know I don't. It's a chance I'm not willing to take. I couldn't live with it on my conscience.'

In truth, she didn't think Stefania would deteriorate to that extent. Although Joseph was concerned about his wife's depression, he'd also told her how strong Stefania had been throughout the process. If she had even one tenth of her brother's strength and determination then Morgan knew she could conquer just about anything.

'And that's the only reason you don't want me to say anything?' Luca asked.

She nodded.

'And Joseph…?' His eyes narrowed on her face. 'Why don't you want me to tell *him* I know about the two of you?'

Morgan dragged in a breath, then released it slowly. 'Come on, Luca. Just for one second assume I'm telling you the truth. If you go to Joseph with these crazy accusations, what do you think he's going to do?'

'Deny it.'

'And…?' she prompted. He knew Joseph as well as she did. Knew how close he and his wife were.

Luca raked a hand through his hair and around the back of his neck. 'And he'd tell Stefania.'

Morgan folded her arms. 'I rest my case.'

* * *

Dio, but this was impossible.

Morgan was still playing with his head.

Black was no longer black.

White was no longer white.

Instead, everything was a murky grey that had the clarity of mud!

While he believed Morgan was genuinely concerned about Stefania's health, her reasoning confirmed neither her guilt nor her innocence.

Luca gritted his teeth until his jaw ached. Clamped his hands into fists until his knuckles turned white.

So what did he do now?

Morgan had accused him several times of being unfair.

Such charges did not sit well with him.

He was a man of honour.

Men of honour had principles.

Principles that included being just and equitable.

His list of reasons for believing Morgan was innocent was now just as long as the one to prove her guilt.

Surely that meant there was room for reasonable doubt?

Grudgingly, Luca had to concede that there was.

But did that mean he was prepared to give Morgan the benefit of the doubt?

No! Not when Stefania's happiness was at stake.

Did that mean he was prepared to get her her job back and forget the whole thing?

No, and no again. Not when there was the slightest chance he could be wrong.

And was he prepared to forget having Morgan as his mistress?

Double, triple, quadruple no. Not when he wanted her more than he'd wanted any woman.

Luca wished he could adopt a neutral position where Morgan was concerned, but he couldn't bring himself to do so.

He had to stick to his guns!

CHAPTER SIX

LUCA INSISTED ON taking her to an Italian restaurant the following evening.

'Have you been here before?' he asked, after the waiter had seated them at an intimate corner table for two.

Morgan laughed. 'I hate to tell you this, Luca, but normal people can't afford to eat in a place like this.'

'I realise that. I just thought someone might have brought you here.'

She tensed, angling her chin into the air, their conversation the previous day still fresh in her mind. 'Someone? Someone like Joseph, perhaps? Is that what you're suggesting?'

Luca frowned across the table at her. 'Actually, I wasn't thinking about Joseph. He wouldn't bring you here. It's too high profile. Too public.'

The implication that Joseph would want to keep their relationship private made the tips of her ears burn. It was obvious Luca still believed she and Joseph were having an affair—despite what she'd told him yesterday.

Overwhelmed by the impossibility of the situation, Morgan thrust back her chair and rose tautly to her feet. 'This isn't going to work. I feel like I'm walking on eggshells all of the time. And all because you're too stubborn to listen to the truth.'

His jaw tightened. 'Sit down, Morgan.'

It was a command. A command she intended to ignore. She shook her head. 'No. Remember condition number one? You're not allowed to tell me what to do!'

He leaned across the table and gently touched her hand. 'Please?'

Morgan stared at the back of his hand. It was covered in scratches. She frowned. 'What happened to your hand?'

'Baci scratched me.'

'Baci...?'

'My sister's cat.'

Her face cleared. Yesterday she'd remained hiding in her bedroom until Luca had finished discussing Joseph before returning to the lounge room. She remembered him telling Stefania he'd check up on her cat for her. 'Is it in a cattery?'

He nodded. 'Yes, I went there this afternoon.' He held up the backs of both hands for her to see. 'This is what I got for my trouble!'

Luca could just as easily have checked on the cat's welfare by making a simple telephone call. She was impressed that he'd taken the time out of his busy schedule to personally ensure Stefania's much loved pet was doing OK.

'What did you do? Pull on its tail?' she asked, looking at the extent of the damage.

Luca shook his head and grinned at her. It was a very boyish grin. 'That wasn't necessary. She took one look at me, arched her spine, and hissed for all she was worth. It was almost as if she knew I was the person responsible for sending her precious mistress away from her.'

Morgan found herself smiling back. 'So can I take it she's not happy where she's staying?'

'That's an understatement! Despite the fact Stefania is paying a small fortune for the place, Baci isn't eating. I tried to coax her into having something but she wasn't having it. You can see what I got for my efforts. Her constant crying is also upsetting the other cats. In the end I had no choice but to take her home with me.'

Her eyebrows shot to her hairline. Contrary to what Luca had just told her, he *had* had a choice. He could have left the cat where it was in the hope the situation would improve. He could even have tried a different cattery.

But he hadn't; he'd taken the cat home.

If she'd wanted evidence of how close Luca was to his sister she'd just received it. And if she'd wanted evidence that Luca was a caring man underneath his arrogant exterior, she'd just received that too.

She cleared her throat. 'What does Baci mean?'

Luca looked from her to her chair and back again. 'Are you going to sit down?'

She swallowed. The sensible thing to do would be to turn around and leave. But she didn't feel like being sensible. Slowly, she resumed her seat.

'Thank you.'

He leaned across the table, his eyes intent on hers. 'I have a suggestion. Let's pretend we've just met. There is no Joseph. Or Stefania. There's just you and me. A man and a woman who are attracted to each other. Because we *are* attracted—aren't we, Morgan?'

His dark eyes blazed with the truth of that statement. Morgan couldn't look away. Nor could she lie. 'Yes. Yes, we are,' she said, her voice little more than a whisper.

He nodded. 'So, let's just forget about everything else and everyone else and enjoy the evening. What do you say?' he asked, holding his hand out across the table.

Morgan wanted to say that he was mad. Crazy.

Make-believe was for children. They were adults.

But then, if Luca was mad then she was too.

Because she wanted nothing more than to do exactly what he'd suggested.

Sucking in a deep breath, she placed her hand in his. The warmth of his fingers closed around hers, strong and somehow reassuring. 'Yes,' she whispered. 'I'd like that.'

Luca sat back, the smile on his face full of warmth and approval. 'Excellent! Do you realise that's the first time we've agreed on something without arguing?'

'Oh, I don't know about that,' Morgan said, trying not to bask in his appreciation. 'We've agreed on other things, too.'

'Like what?'

'Well, you liked the zoo yesterday, didn't you?'

He nodded. 'I did. Particularly the lions.'

'They're my favourites, too.'

He paused for a heartbeat, his eyes locked on her face. 'What else?'

She thought for a moment. 'We both like chocolate. There's nothing surprising about that in my case. I don't think there's a woman alive who doesn't love chocolate. But a lot of men can take it or leave it.'

'How do you know I like chocolate?' he asked, clearly puzzled.

Her lips curved upwards. 'Don't you remember? The other day when you came to my apartment, you helped yourself to a chocolate.'

His face cleared. 'So I did. And why wouldn't I love chocolate? It engages the senses on every level... in much the same way making love to a woman does.' His eyes darkened as he captured her hand, smoothing the inside of her wrist with his thumb. 'For instance, you melt in my arms like pure dark chocolate. And when I kiss you the taste of you lingers on my tongue like the richest caramel-filled chocolate.'

There was something wickedly hypnotic about the way Luca was talking.

'I'm looking forward to finding out what else we have in common,' he said huskily.

Morgan wanted to look away, but she couldn't. 'Me, too.'

Luca leaned back in his chair and picked up the leather bound wine list. 'Would you like a pre-dinner drink?'

'Just wine, please.'

'White or red?'

'I'd prefer red—the heavier the better.'

He raised an eyebrow. 'Really? You surprise me. Most women seem to prefer white.'

'I'm not "most women."'

'You most certainly are not.'

Once again his tone was approving, making her feel warm inside. When he was like this Luca was impossible to resist, Morgan decided, thankful when he turned his attention to the wine list.

A few moments later Luca gestured for the waiter and ordered a Cabernet Sauvignon. 'I think you'll like it.'

'I'm sure I will.'

He was so confident and sure of himself. It made her wonder whether he'd always been that way or whether it was something he'd acquired with age. 'How old are you?' she asked abruptly.

'Thirty-four. And you?'

'Twenty-four.'

'Ten years. That's quite a difference.'

'I suppose it is.'

'Where were you born?'

'Oxford. And you?'

'Rome. What about family? I know your mother is dead. You mentioned that yesterday. But what about your father? Where does he live?'

The question sucked the air from Morgan's lungs. 'My mother never told me who my father was. I believe I'm the product of a one-night stand,' she said carefully.

She didn't want to lie. And she hadn't. At least not outright. Every word she'd spoken was the truth. She'd just omitted to tell Luca that she'd discovered her father's identity after her mother died and had subsequently tracked him down.

'I see. That must have been tough.'

She shrugged. 'It had its moments.'

She said it with such feeling Luca raised an eyebrow.

Even though she felt as though she were tiptoeing on quicksand, Morgan gave in to the temptation to tell Luca about the dream she'd grown up with. 'My mother said I ruined her life. As a result I spent most of my childhood dreaming that my father would turn up one day and take me away. Only he didn't, of course.'

'I'm sorry.'

'Don't be. It wasn't so bad.'

Morgan wanted to share the rest of the story with him. Finding her father had been a special moment in her life. But she swallowed the words back.

She'd wanted to enjoy the evening for what it was, but she was just fooling herself. They could pretend all they liked, but the past wouldn't just go away…

Was that why she'd got involved with Joseph? Luca asked himself. Doing the calculations in his head, he realised that Morgan couldn't have been much more than nineteen or twenty when her mother died.

He remembered feeling lost and alone after the accident. So much so he'd felt quite disorientated.

Had it been the same for Morgan?

Had she been seeking some kind of father figure in Joseph? It was not an unreasonable question, given that he was almost twice her age.

It was tempting to tell himself that that was what had happened. Tempting to forgive her for what she'd done.

But he couldn't afford to start thinking like that. Couldn't afford to let sympathy for her situation soften his attitude.

Not if he wanted to protect Stefania.

Just then the waiter arrived with their wine. Luca welcomed the interruption. He'd meant it when he'd suggested they pretend they'd only just met. He didn't want their situation to constantly intrude on their enjoyment of each other.

After presenting the label for his inspection, the waiter made a production of removing the cork and pouring a small amount into the bottom of Luca's glass for him to try.

Luca swirled the wine around the sides of the glass before lifting it to his nose. He inhaled the full bodied aroma before taking a sip. He savoured the flavour on his tongue before nodding his approval.

He waited for the waiter to fill both of their glasses and depart before raising his glass. '*Salute.*'

Morgan clinked her glass against the side of his. 'Cheers.'

Luca waited while she took a sip. 'What do you think?'

She took her time before answering. 'Hmm. It's nice. It leaves an almost chocolaty taste on the palate.'

He nodded. 'It does. You sound quite knowledgeable.'

She shook her head. 'I'm not. I went to a wine tasting with a group of friends once. They asked questions about each of the wines we tried. The guy from the vineyard labelled me Little Miss Average because most of my answers were wrong.'

Luca liked the fact that Morgan wasn't embarrassed to admit she wasn't an expert, and was even prepared to poke fun at herself. 'The man obviously didn't know what he was talking about. There's nothing average about you. Not a single damned thing.'

She beamed him a smile that made him blink.

A smile should not have that much power, he decided.

A smile like that could turn a man on his head and turn his resolve to water.

After dinner, Luca took her to a fashionable nightclub where he had promised the new owner, a powerful business contact, that he'd make a brief appearance to garner the interest of the A-list-hungry paparazzi.

They didn't linger at the table the waiter miraculously found for them. Luca swept her on to the dance floor with a look that made her mouth run dry.

Morgan went willingly, even eagerly, into his arms.

'Do you like dancing?' he asked huskily, swinging her around on his arm.

'Yes,' she replied breathlessly.

'You see,' he teased, moving effortlessly to the beat, 'we have more in common than you think.'

Luca pulled her closer. Her head tucked neatly under his chin, her cheek turned so that she could hear the not-so-steady beat of his heart.

His mouth feathered a kiss across the crown of her head. She closed her eyes, wrapped her arms around his waist and surrendered to the music.

And to Luca.

Their bodies moved against one another, not so much dancing as making love to a rhythm only they could hear. Luca's body stirred against hers. Hardened. Heat radiated through the clothing separating them, burning into her flesh and triggering an answering response.

Her thighs trembled.

Her nipples tightened into stinging peaks in the confines of her bra.

Heat was drip-fed into her blood stream, warming her from the inside out.

This time his lips brushed across her temple as he put his mouth to her ear. 'Maybe this wasn't such a good idea, after all.'

Feeling his growing arousal against her, Morgan suspected he was right. She looked up, met his eyes, felt the sizzle of desire burn between them. 'You're right,' she whispered. 'I don't think it's a good idea at all.'

But neither of them moved away.

And when his head descended towards hers, Morgan did nothing to stop him, instead lifting her mouth to meet the crush of his.

She was lost from the moment his lips claimed hers.

He dominated her senses to the exclusion of everything else. She was aware of nothing but Luca.

His heat.

His hardness.

The way his mouth moved on hers.

The way his arms held her close.

She clutched his shoulders, her knees so weak she feared they wouldn't support her.

Luca pulled back just far enough to rest his forehead against hers. He was breathing heavily. 'We'd better get out of here before we're arrested.'

'Yes,' she whispered, not thinking about anything but how Luca made her feel.

Alive.

Aroused.

All woman.

And still they didn't move.

Morgan stared deep into Luca's eyes. The gold flecks were burning with heat.

An emotion she didn't recognise stirred inside her. Without thinking, she reached up onto her toes and pressed her mouth against his. It was the first time she'd initiated a kiss between them.

'Luca!'

The voice came from right beside them. Morgan jumped back as if she'd been burned, her face flaming when she saw who it was.

'Olivia,' Luca said. 'What a surprise!'

Morgan glanced sharply at him. There was an edge to his voice. It was subtle, but it was there. It was as if his words were forced in some way.

At first she thought it was because he was uncomfortable having someone from Da Silva Chocolate witness him in a serious clinch.

But then she remembered who she was thinking about.

Luca was confident and assured; he would not be embarrassed so easily.

He met her look with a bland expression, and just like that she knew. Knew that he'd set this up.

Olivia glanced backwards and forwards between them. 'Isn't it?' She spoke pleasantly enough, but there was a hard look in her eyes. 'I didn't expect to see you here, either. And with Morgan. I didn't know the two of you were seeing each other. I thought—' She broke off and issued a false laugh. 'Well, I guess it doesn't matter what I thought.'

As soon as the other woman spoke, it dawned on Morgan that Olivia was Luca's mysterious source. She was surprised she hadn't thought of it before.

Olivia was ambitious. She'd suggested to Joseph several times that he bring the marketing function back in-house for her to manage. Joseph had always vetoed the idea.

With Joseph temporarily out of the picture, had Olivia seen another way of attaining her goal?

Morgan didn't want to think badly of anyone, but her gut instinct warned her that that was exactly what had happened.

She inclined her head. 'No, Olivia. It doesn't matter what you thought.'

She didn't wait for a reply, spinning on her heel and storming off the dance floor. As she departed, she vaguely heard Oliva say, 'Well! What on earth is wrong with Morgan?'

Morgan paused beside their table only long enough to scoop up her handbag. As she pushed through the crowd towards the exit, she thought she heard Luca shout her name, but ignored him.

Tears pricked the backs of her eyes.

Of all the stupid things to do.

Somewhere along the line she'd let herself be seduced into believing the fantasy was real.

Only it wasn't…and never would be.

The scene Luca had just orchestrated proved it!

Luca tried to follow Morgan, but Olivia grabbed hold of his arm. 'If you've got a minute, Luca, I'd like a word with you.'

'Not now.' He didn't even spare her a glance, his eyes focussed on the pitch-black crown of Morgan's head as she wound her way through the crowd towards the door.

The fingers curled like talons around his arm didn't let go. 'It will only take a minute.'

'I said no.'

Without another word, Luca pulled out of her grasp.

He had to follow Morgan.

He'd seen the look on her face.

She knew what he'd done…and she despised him for it.

At that very moment, Luca despised himself.

Which was quite patently ridiculous, of course.

His family had to come first. He had to protect them—no matter what the cost.

Except, he realised, heart twisting, that he wasn't prepared to accept the cost of Morgan running out on their arrangement!

* * *

Morgan didn't get far. She was no more than five paces from the red rope that cordoned off the entrance to the club when a hard hand curled around her shoulder from behind.

'Don't touch me,' she spat, spinning to face him.

'Calm down.'

'No, I won't calm down. I'm so angry, I could hit you.'

'I know you are.'

Morgan stamped her foot. 'Don't agree with me, damn it!'

'Would you rather I disagree with you?'

'That isn't funny.'

'I know it's not.'

The gravity of his tone and the shadow of regret in his eyes made her anger evaporate in a puff of smoke, exposing the raw pain underneath. 'Why, Luca? Why did you do it?'

'You know why.'

Yes, she did. Even though he'd suggested they pretend the past didn't exist, Luca couldn't forget it. 'You brought me here deliberately because you knew Olivia was going to be here, didn't you? You wanted her to see us together because you know she'll tell Joseph—just as she obviously told *you* she'd seen me with Joseph.'

He inclined his head. 'That is correct,' he said, his accent thickening.

'You bastard!'

He shrugged. 'I can assure you that my mother and father were married—even if it was unhappily—at the time of both my conception and my birth.'

She ignored that. 'What I still haven't figured out is

what you hope to achieve. *Why* do you want Joseph to know we've been out together?'

'Because he will never touch you again—not after you have been with me,' Luca replied calmly.

Morgan inhaled sharply. She'd known Luca was ruthless, but had never understood just how ruthless until now. 'You haven't believed a word I've said, have you? I'm just wasting my breath even trying.'

The realisation angered her.

But she also felt incredibly hurt.

With the strength of pent-up emotions, she tore herself out of his arms and stormed off into the night.

Luca watched her march away from him, spine rigid, head held high. He'd hurt her. Really hurt her. He'd seen the shadow of pain cross her face as she'd ripped herself out of his arms.

His chest felt tight. Once again he considered whether he'd made an awful mistake believing Olivia's suspicions. Hadn't he chosen Olivia as the person who would see him with Morgan tonight because he'd instinctively known she'd use the information to her advantage?

But so what?

That didn't mean anything.

She hadn't fabricated what she'd seen. She hadn't lied.

Olivia *had* seen Joseph and Morgan together. Morgan had confirmed that by admitting to those lunches at The Minstrel. Olivia had merely seen an opportunity to benefit herself by revealing what she knew.

Still, Luca couldn't forget the look on Morgan's face just before she'd turned away.

Morgan.

His head snapped up. He'd been so distracted by his thoughts, he'd lost track of her in the crowd. *'Dio!'*

He looked frantically around, and was pleased to see Gino already waiting at the kerb. He flung himself into the back seat and stared through the front windscreen. 'Did you see where she went?'

Gino nodded as he pulled away. 'Round the corner, boss.'

'Step on it.' Luca kept his eyes trained on the pavement, looking for the black flyaway hair, the proud tilt of her head. Finally he saw her. Relief flooded through him. He pointed. 'There she is.'

Gino swerved, ignoring the blast of car horns behind him. Luca leapt from the vehicle before it stopped moving. He planted his feet in the middle of the pavement, barring her way.

Morgan saw him and stopped. She still had that haunted look on her face and his heart wrenched in his chest. 'Get in the car, Morgan.'

She didn't answer him. Instead she turned on her heel and went back in the other direction.

'Damn it, Morgan! It's not safe for you to be wandering the streets at night on your own.'

Frustration drew his shoulders up towards his ears when she kept right on walking. 'If I have to, I'll pick you up and put you in the car myself.'

She stopped and stared at the pavement. She made no move to get in the car.

Luca took a step towards her.

Her head shot up. The look she threw at him as she brushed past him on the way to the car would have frozen the Sahara Desert.

She was so different from the women he'd been

involved with in the past, Luca thought, getting in beside her.

Each and every one of them had been keen and eager to please—to the point where he'd soon grown bored with them.

Morgan was the exact opposite.

She wasn't afraid of telling him exactly what she thought of him.

When he pushed, she shoved straight back.

As he settled back against the leather seat, Luca realised that that was just the way he liked it!

Morgan stared out of the window, not speaking, so angry with Luca she expected steam to pour from her ears at any moment.

Why didn't he listen to reason?

Why didn't he just accept that she and Joseph were friends?

Because he couldn't, she realised, answering her own question.

Luca had mentioned in passing that his mother had had one affair after another. No doubt in his mind there was no smoke without fire.

He was trying to protect his sister. And if that meant manoeuvring the situation to his advantage then that was exactly what he would do.

And could she really blame him for that?

Wasn't she doing exactly the same thing to protect Joseph?

Keeping secrets she didn't want to keep.

Telling lies she didn't want to tell.

She sighed, wishing things were different. Less complicated.

If she'd met Luca under normal circumstances—
No!

Morgan put a brake on her thoughts. There was no point wishing for something that didn't exist. She had to deal with realities, not fantasies.

'I'm sorry I ruined the evening,' Luca murmured into the silence.

Twisting around on her seat, Morgan searched his face. 'Are you really?'

He nodded and picked up her hand, his thumb caressing the tender flesh on the inside of her wrist. 'Yes. I am.' He paused for a heartbeat. 'Please try to understand. I want to believe you. I really do. But Stefania is my only sister. She's too important to me.'

Morgan sighed. Hadn't she just been telling herself exactly that? It might not be right or fair, but it *was* understandable—at least to some extent.

Luca stopped stroking her wrist and clasped her hand. 'If something is going on between the two of you, I had to make sure it has ended. For Stefania's sake. Tonight achieved that. You might not like my methods, but you have to admit that it was the best way to resolve the situation. This way nobody gets hurt. Do you understand?'

Morgan pulled her hands out of his and folded her arms. 'I understand. But you're wrong about nobody being hurt.'

'Am I?

She nodded. 'How do you think *I* feel knowing that you think I'm a liar?'

Luca grimaced. 'Angry and hurt, I suppose.'

'You suppose right,' she said, determined not to wrap it up into something it was not just to make Luca feel better.

He raked a hand over his face. 'I wish things could be different.'

There was no mistaking the sincerity in his voice. His words so closely echoed her own thoughts that tears pricked the backs of her eyes. 'He's always going to come between us, isn't he?' she whispered.

'Only if we let him.' Turning on his seat, he cupped the side of her face and stared deep into her eyes. 'I'm serious, *cara*. We won't talk about it again. We won't even think about it. It's all in the past. Over and done with. What do you say?'

She wanted to say yes.

Wanted to say yes so badly that she could taste it.

But logic suggested that she would be a fool to trust him. She opened her mouth to tell him exactly that. Instead, she pressed her cheek against the palm of his hand and whispered, 'Yes.'

He smiled a slow, warm smile that made his eyes glow. 'Then let us seal our bargain with a kiss,' he said thickly.

When he pulled her into his arms and took her mouth with his Morgan wondered why she was listening to her heart and not her head.

Which, of course, begged another question...

Just when had her heart become involved...?

CHAPTER SEVEN

FROM THAT POINT on life became a fantasy for real, with Luca as her very own Prince Charming.

They didn't discuss the past. Or the future. They just lived for the moment.

The only cloud on the horizon was Joseph. Morgan had overheard part of another conversation between Luca and Stefania—only this time the news hadn't been so good.

It appeared Joseph's medical team were having difficulty getting his blood pressure under control. The specialist Luca had brought in had ordered another series of tests.

The setback sent Morgan's heart plummeting. She felt helpless. All she could do was believe Luca was right when he told Stefania, 'Joseph is in capable hands. He's getting the best care possible. Remember that. Whatever these new test results show, the doctors will deal with it.'

When the weekend arrived, and the weather was half decent, Luca suggested they spend it together in Paris.

'You're kidding, aren't you?' Morgan asked, clutching a hand to her chest. 'Surely it's too late to get airline tickets?'

'We don't have to worry about that,' Luca replied
with a smile. 'I have my own plane. It can be ready to
take off within the hour. All I need is your go-ahead.'

Morgan had taken the ferry over to France as a
teenager, but had never made it as far as Paris. 'I'd love
to go. But where would we stay?'

'I'll book us a hotel suite. With separate bedrooms if
you wish,' he added.

It was on the tip of her tongue to tell him not to
bother about separate rooms, but she swallowed the
words back. Even though she wanted to make love with
Luca more desperately than she'd ever thought possible,
it still troubled her that he'd blackmailed her into
becoming his mistress.

Their agreement hung over her head like a black
cloud. It was a constant reminder of the past they'd
agreed to forget.

But the past seemed very remote as the weekend
turned into a fairytale.

They arrived late on Friday evening. Gino, who had
flown across with them, drove them to their hotel. He
took the circuitous route, so that Morgan could see the
sights, and she spent the journey with her nose pressed
up against the glass.

That evening they dined at their hotel.

Morgan wanted to go for a walk after their meal, but
Luca insisted they have an early night. 'We have a big
day ahead of us tomorrow.'

'Do we? What have you got planned?'

He smiled a heart warming smile. 'It's a secret. You'll
find out tomorrow.'

The next morning they walked hand-in-hand along
the Avenue Montaigne. It took all of thirty seconds for

Morgan to realise this was where the rich and famous bought their clothes.

'What are we doing here?' she asked, clutching Luca's arm. 'When you said you had a big day planned I thought you meant sightseeing.'

'That's next. Right now we're about to buy you an evening dress.'

She stopped, making Luca do the same. 'I don't need an evening dress,' she protested.

'Yes. For the evening I have planned. You do.'

Her breath caught in her throat, her heart leaping in her chest. Eyes locked on his, she reached up on tiptoe and pressed her mouth against his.

Passion flared instantaneously, so much heat and energy flowing between them she half expected sparks to fly at any moment. It wasn't until a wolf whistle pierced the air that they broke apart.

'*Dio,* Morgan! This week cannot be over soon enough,' he rasped. 'I feel as if I am being tortured.'

She dragged in a breath, and then another. 'I know the feeling,' she whispered back.

With every day that passed, Morgan found it harder and harder to resist Luca. He didn't help matters. He seemed to find every excuse to kiss her or touch her or simply pull her into his arms to hold her close.

Their desire had threatened to get out of control on more than one occasion—Morgan was sure they could set the world on fire with the heat they generated between them—but not once had Luca pressured her to sleep with him.

If he had, maybe it would have been easier to resist him. Instead, she found her respect for him growing. He was, she was learning, an honourable and decent man.

Misguided in her case, perhaps, but his heart was certainly in the right place.

'Come on. Let's go and buy you that dress.'

Luca took her hand, but Morgan dug her heels into the pavement. 'It's really not necessary.' She frowned as a thought suddenly occurred to her. 'Unless you're going to be embarrassed if I'm not wearing the right thing.'

He tapped her on the nose with the tip of his finger. 'You would never embarrass me. I'd be proud to take you out wearing jeans, if that's what you want. You'd still be the most beautiful woman there.'

The compliment sent a warm glow through her. 'I don't know,' she said, biting down on her lower lip.

'It's your decision,' Luca said seriously. 'I haven't forgotten what you told me about not ordering you around. But I feel like spoiling you. Please, let me do this for you.'

Morgan knew she should refuse, but somehow she couldn't bring herself to do so. Luca was trying so hard to please her that she didn't have the heart to turn him down. 'All right. But just this once,' she cautioned.

Luca blazed her a smile that made her heart turn over. Then he grabbed her hand and led her into a boutique manned by a uniformed doorman who swung the door open for them.

Luca knew exactly what he wanted. 'The lady would like something long and glamorous in red, please,' he told the elegant assistant who came to serve them.

'I usually wear black,' Morgan interjected quickly.

'But this time you will wear red.'

Again Morgan knew she should object. Luca was being arrogant, thinking he could tell her what to wear. But he seemed to be deriving so much pleasure from being able to buy her something she found herself wanting to please him.

'*Magnifico!*' Luca breathed, sitting up straight in his chair when Morgan appeared in a flame red dress that set off her black hair and magnolia skin to perfection. 'Turn for me,' he said, marking a loop in the air with his finger.

She twirled on high red heels. The skirt swirled around her ankles, its long slit flaring open to reveal a stunning length of toned calf and slender thigh. Nipped in at the waist, the dress outlined the feminine flare of her hips and the fullness of her breasts. His eyes lingered on the hint of cleavage revealed by the low neckline, then lifted to her face.

His heart contracted, his breath catching in the back of his throat. 'You are one very beautiful woman, Morgan Marshall.'

Her cheeks flamed.

Luca frowned. This was not the first time she'd acted embarrassed when he'd paid her a compliment. Luca liked the fact that she didn't consider such flattery her due. She didn't primp and preen, and she wasn't vain. It made him realise how shallow some of his previous lovers had been.

But her reaction did make him wonder. It was as if she wasn't used to receiving male admiration. But he could hardly believe her past lovers had been remiss in paying tribute to her beauty.

Luca ruthlessly reined in his thoughts. He didn't want to think along those lines. Didn't want anything to ruin this weekend for them.

The past was in the past. Let it stay there.

If this was a fantasy, he was more than happy for it

to continue. Each day he spent with her was better than the one before. Each time he left her, he couldn't wait to get back to her.

'We'll take it,' he instructed.

Afterwards, they strolled along the Avenue des Champs-Elysées, where they stopped for a coffee and Morgan took almost fifteen minutes to select a cake from the delectable array artfully arranged in the glass window.

'I've always wanted to visit Paris,' Morgan said, sighing blissfully as she licked the last crumbs of cake off her lips. 'And Rome. You said you were born in Rome. Do you go there often?'

He shook his head. 'I haven't been back to Italy since moving to London after the accident.'

'Oh.' Her eyes softened with sympathy. 'I often wondered why you weren't based in Italy.'

'Well, now you know.' He dragged in a deep breath. 'Now, if you've finished your coffee, we should get going. We still have the Arc de Triomphe, the Luxembourg Gardens, the Eiffel Tower, the Nôtre Dame Cathedral and the Louvre to see.'

Luca had seen all of these tourist destinations before, most of them more than once. But seeing them with Morgan turned them into a brand new experience.

She had a genuine appreciation for everything he showed her.

Her pleasure became his pleasure.

Her enjoyment his.

He loved watching her smile.

And laugh.

And he was delighted when she 'ooh'd' and 'ah'd' or when she grabbed his arm in excitement and gasped, 'Look at that, Luca. Isn't it beautiful?'

He would say, 'Yes, it certainly is,' but in his mind the most beautiful thing he saw was her. She took his breath away.

With every day that passed, Luca found it more and more difficult to believe she'd ever had an affair with Joseph. The neutral stance he'd found so difficult to take now felt a lot more comfortable. So much so he dreaded anything happening to challenge his position.

If he ever had to commit one way or another he was going to be in one hell of a lot of trouble!

Luca smiled as he rang Morgan's doorbell. He was looking forward to seeing her.

Last night, on their return from Paris, he hadn't wanted to leave her. And today he hadn't been able to stop thinking about her. He'd even found himself doodling her name on his notepad during a meeting, which was something he'd never done before.

Something else he'd never done before was postpone an important business trip for a woman. And yet that was exactly what he'd done with his US visit—rescheduled it for the second time this week so that he could be with Morgan.

He frowned at the door. Morgan should have answered by now.

He'd tried calling her several times during the afternoon, but her phone had diverted to voicemail. He'd left her several messages but she hadn't called back.

He rang the bell again, and this time was rewarded with the sound of the lock turning. The door opened. Morgan was framed in the doorway. She was wearing his favourite black I'm-in-charge leather boots, with a cream suit and a black blouse.

'You didn't check to see who it was before you opened the door,' he reprimanded, stepping forward to gather her in his arms so that he could kiss her hello.

She backed out of his reach before he could touch her. 'I forgot,' she said unsmilingly. Turning on her heel, she walked back into the apartment, leaving him to follow.

Luca took his time, frowning at her rigid back. 'I'm serious, Morgan. I don't want anything to happen to you. Check next time.'

She nodded, but didn't answer him.

His frown deepened. Morgan was the antithesis of the woman who'd kissed him goodnight on their return from Paris.

That woman had been glowing with happiness. Pleasure had shone from her eyes like rays of sunshine and her smile had been powerful enough to light up the night sky.

Luca had felt his chest swell with pride to know *he'd* put that smile on her face.

Morgan wasn't smiling now.

Her face wasn't glowing, either. Instead she was pale, her expression pinched, her eyes dull and flat.

His heart turned over in his chest, a sinking feeling attacking his stomach. 'What's wrong?'

She folded her arms. 'Nothing.'

Luca knew that tone. He'd heard it before. It was cold enough to freeze the Sahara. 'Don't tell me nothing is wrong when it's as plain as the nose on your face that you're upset about something!'

Her face twisted. 'I don't want to talk about it.'

What could have happened between yesterday and today to make her this upset? Luca asked himself, his insides contracting into a tight ball of knots.

His brain clicked into gear as he pieced together what he knew. 'I tried calling you today but there was no answer in the apartment,' he said, thinking out loud. 'You didn't answer your mobile, either.' His gaze sharpened on her face. 'Where were you?'

'Out.'

Her monosyllabic answer deepened his anxiety until it felt as though invisible hands were squeezing around his throat. 'Out where?'

Morgan tossed her head, sending her hair swirling around her shoulders. 'Are you checking up on me?'

Luca's frown deepened. She was as prickly as a porcupine. To say she was in a strange mood would be an understatement. 'No. I'm merely curious to know where you were this afternoon. Is there anything wrong with that?'

'I suppose not.' She stared at him for a long moment. Luca could practically hear the cogs of her mind turning over. Finally she angled her chin into the air, her eyes glittering like black diamonds. 'If you must know, I had a job interview this afternoon.'

Luca tensed at the mention of what he knew was a sensitive subject. 'I didn't know you were still looking for a new job. You haven't mentioned it.'

She gave him a tight smile that didn't reach her eyes. 'Why would I when you're the person responsible for having me fired me in the first place? Unjustifiably, I might add.'

It was the first reference either of them had made to the past in days. The atmosphere in the room thickened, the silence taking on a quality that prickled at the back of his neck.

Luca stared at her, and his discomfiture increased. The way she was looking at him, black eyes full of challenge, forced him to confront once again the possibility that he was wrong about her.

If he was then he had indeed treated her unfairly.

Tension lifted his shoulders towards his ears. His heart was so heavy it felt as if he'd swallowed a rock.

'And how did the interview go?' he asked, carefully avoiding any mention of his role in her current situation.

'I thought it went well, but they've had a lot of applicants. I'm up against some pretty tough competition.'

'I see.' Luca walked over to the kitchen and poured himself a whisky and a red wine for Morgan. 'It isn't necessary for you to find another job, you know. I can give you an allowance.'

She shook her head stubbornly. 'No, thank you. I like paying my own way. And, besides, I'd be bored to tears with nothing to do all day.'

This was not the first time Morgan had turned down money from him. She'd thrown his cheque back in his face that first day in the office. Since then she'd also refused several gifts of jewellery, claiming she didn't feel comfortable accepting something so expensive. He'd virtually had to twist her arm to get her to accept the dress he'd bought her in Paris.

And now this.

It was a new experience for him. His past mistresses had been more than happy to take whatever they could get from him—sometimes throwing out not-so-subtle hints if they didn't think he was being generous enough.

Luca sat down on the couch and motioned for Morgan to join him. 'I thought you women liked to shop.'

'Maybe. But I couldn't shop all day. I couldn't afford to, for one thing. I also happen to like working.'

Luca remembered back to one of the first conversations they'd ever had. 'How are you coping with your mortgage?'

She laughed. It was a harsh sound that grated on his eardrums like fingernails on a blackboard. 'I've had to ask my bank for a temporary halt to my repayments until I find a new job.'

'I see.' His heart contracted until it felt the size of a pea. Guilt ate into him like acid into stone. 'Would you like me to take over the repayments for you? Or pay the mortgage off outright? Then you won't need to worry.'

Even before he'd finished speaking she was shaking her head. 'No. I won't take money from you.'

Her answer made a shiver run up and down his spine.

The crack that had appeared in his belief that she'd had an affair with Joseph had just got one hell of a lot wider. It was impossible to imagine that her values where money was concerned weren't carried over into the other areas of her life.

Not wanting to think about what that implied, Luca asked, 'Would you like me to ask around? See if I can find a position for you?'

She shook her head. Then, after a moment's hesitation, she said, 'You could always get me my old job back.'

Luca tensed. 'Please don't ask me to do that.'

'Why? Because your answer will be no?'

Luca didn't answer her.

She laughed bitterly. 'We agreed to put the past behind us, but all I have to do is scratch below the surface to find you think no better of me now than you did before. It doesn't matter what I say or do, you're never going to change your opinion of me, are you?'

'That's not true,' Luca protested, but it was a weak protest and they both knew it.

He hadn't wanted his neutral position to be tested. By asking him to get her her old job back Morgan had just done exactly that.

The hell of it was, it was a test he'd failed…!

Although Morgan didn't want to go out after that, Luca insisted.

She acquiesced, but the remote look in her eyes suggested she was a long way from forgiving him.

Luca set out to be his most charming. And it worked. By the time coffee was served she'd thawed sufficiently to actually smile once or twice.

They were on their way back to her apartment when Gino suddenly slammed on the brakes. Their car skewed sideways as he pulled hard on the steering wheel to avoid hitting the navy blue sedan in front of them.

Luca acted on instinct, thrusting an arm across Morgan as they were flung forward against their seat belts.

Memories of that long ago accident rushed to the surface. It had been dark that night, too. The sound of metal screeching against metal had rent the air, just as it did now.

His heart was racing, slamming against his ribcage, his skin breaking out in a cold sweat. Images flashed into his head at kaleidoscopic speed. His mother and father slumped in their seats. Blood everywhere. Stefania screaming.

He began to shake.

He couldn't move.

He couldn't think.

He might physically be in the car…but the rest of him was firmly fixed in the past.

Then he heard movement beside him.

Morgan!

In a flash, he was transported back to the present.

He had to get a grip. He was of no use to anyone—Morgan, Gino, the people in the car up ahead—if he didn't get himself back under control.

Dragging in a breath, he turned towards Morgan, terrified of what he might find.

She looked pale and shaken, but otherwise appeared OK.

'Are you all right?' he asked, squeezing the words out through numb lips.

She nodded.

'Gino?' Luca prompted as he rapidly removed his seat belt and moved closer to Morgan.

'I'm fine, boss.'

Looking at the carnage through the front windscreen, it took Luca a few moments to figure out what had happened. A car travelling on the cross street had run straight through a red light into the car ahead.

'Call the police and an ambulance,' Luca instructed as he unsnapped Morgan's seat belt and began running his hands over her. He wasn't sure what he was looking for. He just knew that he had to make sure she was OK.

If something happened to her…

His heart beat even more frantically against his breastbone, his mind shutting down on the rest of that thought.

'What are you doing?' Morgan asked.

'Checking for injuries.'

She swatted his hands away. 'I told you. I'm all right. But I don't think the people in the car up ahead have been so lucky. We have to help them.'

Before Luca could stop her, Morgan had pushed open her door and was running towards the sedan. He sat frozen for one moment, then went after her, aware from the sounds behind him that Gino had finished calling the authorities and was following them.

What followed was a nightmare. A nightmare that seemed to unfold in slow motion so that the horror of it impacted more deeply.

Luca had another bad moment when he realised that the sedan was not only carrying two adults but two children, one of whom was a young girl not much older than Stefania had been when she'd been injured all those years ago. He felt his composure beginning to crack, and it took every ounce of his will-power to rein it back in and do what he had to do.

Morgan gravitated towards the children. Luca did what he could for the parents, both of whom were in pretty bad shape, while they waited for the paramedics.

Gino was nowhere to be seen. Luca assumed he was attending to the occupants of the car that had run the red light.

After what seemed like hours, but was probably only several minutes, the police and an ambulance arrived with sirens blaring. Suddenly there were people everywhere.

Because a fatality was involved—the driver of the vehicle running the red light hadn't made it—there were questions.

Lots and lots of questions.

Luca kept Morgan tucked in close to his side as they gave their statement. Every now and then a tremor made her body shake. Finally he'd had enough. His mouth tightened. 'That will be all for now, gentlemen. Ms Marshall has been through quite an ordeal this evening. It's time I took her home.'

Her head swung in his direction. 'I'm all right, Luca.'

Luca searched her face. She was pale. There were purple smudges beneath her eyes and a white ring of tension around her mouth. He shook his head. 'You are not all right. You are exhausted.'

The officer in charge smiled ingratiatingly. 'Just a couple more questions, Mr da Silva, and then you'll be free to leave.'

Luca turned on him, a warning look in his eyes. 'No. No more questions. Not tonight.' He fished a business card out of his pocket. 'If you present yourself at this address tomorrow morning, we'll be more than happy to tell you whatever you want. But tonight we've had enough.'

The policeman looked from Luca's determined face to the slender female figure tucked protectively at his side and nodded. 'I'll call you.'

Luca led Morgan to the car. 'Are you OK to drive?' he asked Gino, who nodded and got in behind the wheel. 'Kensington,' he said, and Gino inclined his head to acknowledge their change of destination.

Luca handed Morgan into the back seat and strode around to join her, sitting in the centre and putting an arm around her shoulders.

'Are you OK?' he asked.

Her skin was cold. She was shaking. 'Y…yes. I'm fine.'

His top teeth met his bottom ones with a snap. Fine? She was far from being fine. Now that it was over, reaction was setting in.

'I just…' She shook her head. 'Those poor children.'

He hugged her to his side. 'I know. But they're in good hands. I'm sure they'll be OK.'

She nodded.

Luca pulled her more closely against him. She turned so that her cheek rested on his shoulder for the remainder of the journey.

'We're here,' Luca said quietly as they pulled up in his private driveway.

She started. Looked around. Nodded.

But she didn't ask where they were—proof in his mind that she was in shock.

Luca helped her out of the car and up the stairs. Gino was already holding the door open for them.

'*Grazie,* Gino. That will be all.'

Luca half-urged, half-carried Morgan along the corridor to his bedroom. Not once did he consider putting her in one of the guestrooms. He wanted to keep an eye on her.

It wasn't until he'd closed the door behind them that Morgan finally woke from the haze that had been holding her captive since the accident.

'Where are we?' she asked, looking around.

Luca tossed his jacket over the back of a chair. 'We're in my apartment.'

Her head swung in his direction so hard and fast Luca was surprised she hadn't strained a muscle. 'Your apartment? What are we doing here?'

He took her handbag and deposited it on the same chair as his jacket, then smoothed a strand of black hair away from her strained face. 'You shouldn't be alone tonight. You've had a shock.'

'I'll be all right,' she protested, but it was a weak protest and they both knew it.

'I'm sure you will be,' Luca said calmly, stroking a finger down the side of her cheek. 'But I'd rather keep an eye on you.'

The truth of that statement reverberated deep inside him. Even if she'd had a close relative he could have taken her to he knew he wouldn't have done so. He didn't trust anyone else to take care of her.

She nodded. 'OK.'

Of their own volition his hands massaged the curves of her shoulders. 'The bathroom is through there,' he said, nodding his head towards the left. 'I'm sure you'd like a shower.'

'Yes, please.' She frowned. 'What about you?'

'I'll shower in one of the guest bathrooms. Then I'll get us something to drink. How does tea sound? Or would you prefer something stronger?'

She shook her head. 'Tea will be fine.' She started to turn away, only to swing back towards him, hands clasped together in front of her. 'Do you think we can call the hospital and see how the family are doing?'

Something squeezed tight in his chest. Instinct made him pull her towards him. She fitted just under his chin as if they'd been designed that way. He inhaled the citrus tang of her shampoo. 'Of course. I'll do that as soon as I've showered.'

It was a thoughtful Luca who left the room.

He was, he decided, a fool.

A blind fool.

The truth had been staring him in the face all along.

From the minute Morgan had tossed his cheque back at him he should have known. Known she was not the kind of woman to have an affair with a married man.

He felt the truth of that statement resound deep inside of him.

She'd been telling him the truth, only he'd been too blinkered to see it. Now her innocence was crystal-clear.

Despite the tragedy of the evening, Luca felt as if a weight had been lifted off him.

He could hardly wait to tell Morgan.

But not tonight.

Tonight she needed to rest and recover.

Tomorrow he would tell her.

He would take her somewhere special for dinner. He would shower her with flowers and chocolates. Afterwards he would take her in his arms and tell her that he believed her.

He frowned. That was not all he had to do, he realised. He also had to undo the damage he had done.

He would get her her old job back, if that was what she wanted. If not, he'd find her a new one.

But first and foremost he had to release her from their agreement.

Tell her that she was free to leave whenever she wanted to go.

And then he would ask her to be his mistress.

Not because she had to.

But because she wanted to.

CHAPTER EIGHT

MORGAN STEPPED THROUGH the bedroom door wrapped in a huge towel, with another twisted turban-style around her head.

Luca was just setting down a tray on the bedside table. He was wearing a black robe shot with gold and a pair of black slippers. Between the lapels she could see a triangle of golden skin dusted with fine dark hair.

Her mouth ran dry when she realised he was naked under the robe. Clutching her hand to her breast, as much to stop the frenetic race of her heart as to stop the towel from slipping, she said in a voice that hardly sounded like her own, 'I don't have anything to wear.'

Luca pointed to the bed. 'You have a choice. One of my T-shirts or one of my business shirts. Take your pick.'

She picked up a T-shirt and disappeared back into the bathroom to get changed.

'Did you call the hospital?' she asked when she emerged a second time.

Luca nodded, face grim. 'The father is in surgery. The mother and two children are in a serious but stable condition.'

The tension that had compressed her insides into a

mass of knots relaxed. Ridiculously, her eyes filled with tears. 'Thank God for that!'

'My sentiments exactly,' Luca said grim-faced. 'When I saw those children…'

For the first time since the accident, Morgan looked at Luca properly, and was stunned by what she found. He looked tired, with lines of tension ringing his mouth and nose.

She slapped the centre of her forehead with the palm of her hand, her tears forgotten. 'I'm so sorry, Luca. How stupid of me! I didn't think about how this must have affected you. Tonight must have brought back memories of the accident that killed your parents.'

Luca nodded, face tense. 'It did. As soon as I heard the sound of metal on metal, it all came flooding back.'

Her heart wrenched. She hurried over to him, taking both of his hands in hers. 'I'm sorry, Luca. You must think I'm as insensitive as a plank of wood.'

He smiled and squeezed her hands. 'No. I don't think you're insensitive at all.' His eyes dropped the length of her as he added huskily, 'And you don't resemble a plank of wood in the least.'

His response melted her heart. Taking a big breath, she asked quietly, 'Will you tell me what happened?'

She half expected him to make some kind of sarcastic comment about Joseph having told her the details, but all he said was, 'Let's have some tea first.'

He filled two mugs from an ornate silver teapot and then sat down on the bed, his long hair-roughened legs stretched out in front of him.

He patted the covers beside him. 'Come and have your tea.'

Morgan hesitated for only a second before going and

sitting down beside him, tugging on the hem of his T-shirt, which barely reached mid-thigh.

Luca handed her a steaming mug. Morgan took it and blew across the surface before taking a sip of the strong, sweet brew. She was about to ask him about the accident when a chocolate brown cat leapt on to the bed, padded across her legs and promptly sat down in her lap.

'Who's this?' She scratched the cat behind the ears and was rewarded with a contented purr.

'Baci.'

'Stefania's cat?' Morgan said.

'Yes. You should consider yourself privileged. This is the first time she's come anywhere near me since I brought her home. The staff have been looking after her.'

'She's gorgeous,' Morgan murmured. 'You never did tell be what Baci means.'

'Kisses.'

'What a delightful name.'

'I suppose it is.'

Morgan took another sip of her tea, stroking the cat with her spare hand. 'Tell me about the accident.'

Luca was silent, as if he was gathering his thoughts. 'It was dark that night, too. My parents were fighting—as usual. They fought a lot, you know.'

Morgan shook her head. 'No, I didn't know.'

'My father accused my mother of having another affair.' He barked out a harsh laugh. 'She had a lot of those. They argued. My father wasn't concentrating. He drifted into oncoming traffic.'

Morgan pressed shaking fingers to her mouth. 'Oh, no.'

She wasn't sure Luca even heard her.

'The truck that hit us was travelling at speed. My parents were killed instantly.'

Suppressing a gasp, Morgan put a hand on his forearm, not surprised to find it rigid with tense muscles.

'The impact pushed in the rear passenger door so hard that the metal fractured inwards, straight into Stefania's stomach,' he said, talking in an unemotional tone that somehow made the impact of his words cut all the deeper.

This time Morgan couldn't suppress the gasp that escaped her strangled throat. 'I'm so sorry, Luca. So very, very sorry.'

He turned and looked at her, face grim, eyes bleak. '*Si*, so am I. I should have stopped it from happening.'

'No!' Morgan pushed Baci off her lap and scooted around until she was facing him, her hand squeezing tight on his arm. 'You mustn't say that.'

He laughed, but it was a harsh sound. 'Why not? Because it's true. I was seventeen. I could have done something. I *should* have done something.'

She pressed her fingers against his lips and shook her head vehemently. 'No. You can't take responsibility for what happened. It was an accident. A tragic accident.'

She could see by the look on his face that he didn't believe her.

And suddenly it all clicked into place.

The accident was the reason Luca was so over-protective of Stefania. He felt he'd failed her once and was determined not to let it happen again.

That was why he interfered in his sister's marriage; he probably didn't even realise he was doing it.

And that was why he'd been so willing to believe that she and Joseph were having an affair—because he couldn't risk being wrong.

Her heart twisted tight.

'Luca—'

She broke off, not sure what she'd planned on saying to him. Luca had been carrying a burden on his shoulders that he should never have had to carry. She wanted to say something to make him see that the accident wasn't his fault, but other than what she'd already said there was nothing she could say.

But there was one thing she *could* do.

She could tell him the truth, so that he could finally put to bed his concerns about Stefania's marriage.

But now was not the time.

They were both shocked and tired.

They needed a good night's sleep.

They needed something else, too.

'What?' Luca asked when she failed to continue.

She stared him in the eye. 'Make love to me.'

He gasped. 'Why? Because you feel sorry for me?' He shook his head. 'I don't think so.'

'I don't feel sorry for you. I think you're crazy for thinking the accident was your fault.'

'Then why?'

She picked up his hand and brought it to her breast. 'Because I want you.'

He shook his head again. 'You're in shock.'

'No, I'm not. Or at least not abnormally so. I know what I'm saying. The accident reminded me that life is short. I don't want to waste our time together.'

His eyes searched her face, but he made no move towards her.

She smiled a wobbly smile. 'I didn't think that when I finally surrendered you wouldn't want me any more.'

'Oh, I want you. Make no mistake about that,' Luca said in a carefully controlled voice. 'Saying no, sitting here and not touching you, is one of the hardest things I've ever had to do.'

She frowned. 'Then why do it? Why not just say yes?'

'Because the week isn't up. I made you a promise. I intend to keep it.'

Screwing up her courage, Morgan grasped the hem of his T-shirt between her fingers and pulled it up over her head, flicking it away to land who knew where. The turban-like towel went with it, her hair tumbling down around her naked shoulders and breasts. 'I want you now.'

She could barely breathe as she waited for his response. She had never done anything so blatantly provocative before. She would be mortified if he rejected her.

A smile spread slowly across his face. 'Then who am I to resist?' he said, taking hold of her hand and tugging her towards him so that she fell across his chest.

His arms came around her, holding her close.

It was then, with his heart beating out its power and energy against her that Morgan realised she'd fallen in love with him.

Luca rolled over, tumbling her onto her back beneath him. Then he leaned up on one elbow and just looked at her.

She was magnificent.

Miles of clear magnolia skin gleamed in the lamplight, just begging to be stroked and kissed.

He smoothed the silken length of her hair down between her breasts, admiring the contrast of black against white.

Her breasts were full and rounded. He cupped one with his hand. Her skin was smooth and soft and warm. He brushed the pad of his thumb across her nipple and was rewarded when it immediately contracted into a tightly erect bead.

'You have beautiful breasts,' he whispered huskily, turning his attention to the other one. 'So responsive.'

He put his mouth to the sensitive column of her throat. She quivered.

He kissed his way down to her breast, where his cupped hand made an offering of it, and took the nipple into his mouth, rolling it around on his tongue.

She shuddered and clutched at his shoulders.

He kept on kissing his way down her body, tracing the bottom of her ribcage with his tongue, then sweeping an erotic circle around her navel. Her stomach muscles contracted as she gasped for breath.

Her fingers dug into his hair. At first Luca thought she was going to push him away. Instead she clung to him as his mouth left a series of tiny kisses on her belly.

His fingers found the nest of curls at the apex of her thighs, seeking the tiny bud that controlled the centre of her pleasure. She began to buck against his hand, her breath coming in gasps.

He explored further, finding the slick, wet heat of her.

She lifted her hips off the bed. 'Luca—'

'I know,' he soothed, kissing his way back up her body. 'I always knew you would be like this. You are bursting with passion in the same way a peppermint cream or a cherry liqueur chocolate is bursting with flavour. One bite and your senses explode.'

'Am I?'

He lifted his head and nodded. 'Touch me,' he ordered, his body so taut and tight he thought he might explode at any moment.

She did. Tentatively at first, as though she wasn't used

to touching a man. And then she seemed to gain confidence, her hands stroking his flesh, kneading his muscles.

And then it was his turn to shudder.

He took her mouth with his. She tasted hot and sweet, and a shot of pure need fired through his body. He caressed her until she sobbed out his name. Sucked on her nipples until her head thrashed from side to side on the pillow and she was begging him to take her.

He lifted his head. 'Look at me.'

Her thick, dark lashes fluttered open, revealing eyes glazed with passion.

Then and only then did he thrust inside her, with one smooth, bold stroke. She was tight. He withdrew slowly, then thrust in deeper.

And then he wasn't thinking at all.

All he could do was feel.

Sensation spiralled rapidly out of control, spinning him to a place he'd never been before.

It felt as if he'd been waiting for this moment for ever. And in the sweet aftermath of passion, as he lay with his head on her breast, Luca realised that Morgan had been worth the wait.

Two weeks later Morgan let herself into Luca's apartment with the key he'd given her and headed straight for the shower, undressing as she went.

Given that Luca had once told her he never lived with his mistresses, she was surprised *she* was still living there. She kept waiting for him to suggest she return to her own apartment, but he never did.

And, since she enjoyed sleeping in his arms every night, neither did she.

She'd kept quiet about something else, too.

Two somethings, actually.

Just yesterday she'd been thrilled to receive a phone message from Joseph.

He'd apologised for not being in contact with her before now. He'd explained how Luca had sprung the trip on them as a surprise, giving him no chance to call and warn her of his departure.

Morgan had almost cried when she'd heard his voice; he'd sounded just like his normal self.

He hadn't mentioned his heart attack, but then she wouldn't have expected him to—he'd know it would only worry her.

He'd finished the message by telling her that he loved her and would be home soon.

The other thing she hadn't told Luca was the truth about her relationship with Joseph.

Every day she kept putting if off.

At first she'd justified the delay by telling herself she had to speak to Joseph first. But as the weeks progressed she'd realised she had to do no such thing.

Joseph shouldn't have asked her to keep their relationship a secret. She'd grown up with a mother who had been ashamed of her existence and had treated her like a poor second all of her life. Joseph knew all that, and yet he'd done exactly the same thing.

Acted as if she was something to hide. Treated her as if she wasn't important enough in his life to tell everyone about.

Sure, he had his reasons. She understood that.

But what about *her?* What about what *she* wanted? What about *her* rights?

She'd done nothing wrong. Joseph was the one who had slept with one woman while engaged to another. It was time he stood up and took ownership of what he'd done.

No doubt the stress of keeping their relationship a secret had contributed towards his heart attack. Getting everything out in the open could be just the release he needed.

And she should stand up for who she was and be proud enough to shout it from the rooftops.

If she'd done that in the first place then she wouldn't be in this mess.

Not that it felt like a mess.

It felt anything but.

Being with Luca made her feel whole in a way she'd never felt before. He made her life complete.

Every day just got better and better.

She didn't want to ruin that.

What if she told Luca the truth and he wanted nothing more to do with her?

What was the saying about the sins of the father being visited on his sons? Or in this case his daughter? Even though she'd done nothing wrong, her mother had blamed her existence for ruining her life.

Whether she was innocent of any wrongdoing or not, she was still a physical representation of Joseph's betrayal. Still a symbol of his unfaithfulness. Luca was so over-protective of Stefania. Wasn't it feasible he'd want to get her as far away from his sister as possible to save her from being hurt?

Her heart contracted on a spasm of pain. What if—?

A sound made her look up.

Luca was lounging in the open doorway, watching her.

Morgan swiped her wet hair off her face. 'Hi. How was your day?'

'Lonely. I missed you.'

Her mouth curved up in a smile. 'Did you? But you only saw me this morning.'

Luca tugged off his tie and dropped it on the floor. 'I know. It was a *long* day.'

She laughed. 'It's only three o'clock. You should still be at work.'

He unbuttoned his shirt and shrugged it off, baring a broad expanse of smooth golden skin quilted with muscle. He raised an eyebrow. 'Are you trying to get rid of me?'

Her mouth ran dry. 'No. What are you doing?' she asked, when his belt buckle parted and his zip slid down.

'What does it look like I'm doing?'

'Getting undressed.'

His trousers slid down his hips and joined the growing pile of clothing on the tiled floor. His black underpants did little to hide the growing state of his arousal.

'That's right. I thought I'd take a shower.'

Heat was drip-fed into her blood stream at the thought of him joining her. A pulse between her thighs throbbed. 'Did you?'

'*Si*. I trust you have no objection?' He smiled a slow, sexy smile and raked his eyes over her in a searing look that had the same intensity as a thousand caressing fingers stroking her skin.

'None,' she said, barely able to speak.

His underpants dropped to the floor, leaving his engorged flesh naked to her hungry gaze. Her internal organs quivered as Luca pushed open the shower door. She licked her lips and backed up against the tiles.

'I love the way you lick your lips like that,' he murmured huskily. 'It turns me on so hard, I can hardly wait to be inside of you.'

She pressed her hands against his chest, then raised

up on tiptoes to brush a kiss across the curve of his mouth. 'Then I'd better make sure I lick them all the time,' she whispered, tossing her head back.

Luca laughed and angled his mouth against the exposed column of her throat. 'You do that and we'll *never* get out of bed.'

What followed blew her mind—and everything else!

Luca's hands and mouth were everywhere. He cupped her breasts and rolled her nipples between his thumb and finger until she writhed against him. His fingers trailed down over her abdomen and into the nest of curls at the apex of her thighs.

She groaned as one of his fingers slid inside her. When it was joined by another, her knees buckled.

Luca flung his head back and laughed. It was a triumphant laugh. But Morgan didn't care. She dug her hands into the wet hair on either side of his head and tugged his mouth back to hers.

This time it was Luca's turn to shudder. He picked her up, pressed her back against the wall and thrust inside her. Morgan wrapped her legs around his hips. He cupped her bottom.

Luca lifted his head. 'I love making love to you. You are so passionate, you blow my mind.'

'Better than chocolate?' Morgan gasped.

'Much better than chocolate,' he husked, thrusting inside her with an increasing rhythm until the world splintered apart.

As he carried her through to the bedroom, Morgan realised she couldn't put off telling him the truth any longer.

It wasn't fair.

To him.

Or to her.

She would tell him…just as soon as the time was right.

Luca woke to the feel of a soft and warm female body curled around him. He smiled and carefully rolled over.

Morgan was still sound asleep, her hair spread in wild disarray across the pillow, one arm thrown over his waist, the other tucked beside her head.

Unable to resist, Luca reached out and stroked a strand of hair off her face. *Dio,* but she was magnificent. Lured by the lush ripeness of her mouth and the smell of warm female flesh all around him, he bent his head and kissed her.

She stirred.

He smiled…and kissed her again.

Her lashes fluttered against her cheeks.

He kissed her again.

She opened her eyes.

And then she smiled at him.

Her smile was like a ray of sunshine or a rainbow after a summer storm. Pleasure burst to life inside of him. *'Buongiorno, cara.'*

'Good morning,' she replied huskily.

He rolled over and was rewarded by a loud, un-friendly hiss.

He looked down the bed. Baci had been asleep, lying on top of the covers between them. His sudden movement had woken her. She gave him her usual baleful look.

'Get lost, cat,' Luca said, nudging it with his knee.

He was rewarded with another hiss, before the cat raised itself up onto its paws, turned and pranced off the bed with its tail in the air.

'Now…where were we?' Luca asked, rolling over and pinning her body beneath him. His flesh began to swell in instant, gut-wrenching response. 'You are wearing me out,' he said thickly.

'I'm not doing anything,' she protested with a smile.

He laughed, only to stop when he saw the way she was looking at him. '*Dio,* Morgan,' he groaned, bending his head to kiss her. 'I can't get enough of you.'

One kiss led to another in a fevered hunger that drove Luca to the very edge of his control. Never before had he struggled to suppress his own climax so that his partner could achieve pleasure first.

'I can't wait,' he said hoarsely, positioning himself between her spread thighs. 'You drive me insane.'

'Do I?' She smiled and fed her hands into the hair on either side of his head. 'I kind of like that idea.'

'Do you?' he asked, barely able to speak.

'Uh-huh. Because you drive me insane, too.'

'Now, *that* I definitely like.'

But in the sweet aftermath of passion, as he lay in his lover's arms, Luca realised he was living a lie.

He still hadn't told Morgan what she deserved to hear: that he knew she'd been telling him the truth all along.

And that was wrong.

He lived by a code he couldn't ignore.

Honour had to come before lust.

Duty had to come before pleasure.

Just because he was unsure of Morgan's reaction it was no excuse.

He had to do the right thing.

He couldn't put off telling her any longer.

As soon as the time was right, he would arrange a special dinner for them.

Then he would tell her that he believed her.

* * *

A sound in the doorway made Luca look up from the papers he was signing. His sister, elegant as always in a tan trouser suit, was framed in the doorway.

'Stefania!' he exclaimed, rising to his feet and rounding the desk. 'What are you doing here?'

She flung her hands in the air, a broad smile on her face. 'Surprise!'

'It certainly is.' He took her hands in his and kissed her on both cheeks. 'You're supposed to be in Australia.'

'I know. But Joe's heart attack put a bit of a dampener on things.' She paused, then added, 'We had a long talk while he was in hospital.'

Luca frowned. 'What about?'

'About a lot of things. Some of which happened a long time ago and I can't tell you about just yet.'

'That sounds very mysterious.'

She nodded. 'It is. We also made a major decision.'

'And that is?'

'We're going to fill in the papers for adoption today.'

Luca frowned. 'Really? I thought you didn't want that. I thought you were determined to have your own child.'

She shrugged. 'I was. But at some point I have to face reality. It isn't going to happen.'

'It might,' he said, his insides tight and tense. This was his fault. If he'd done something to prevent the accident then Stefania would not be in this situation. 'You just—'

'Shush.' She pressed her fingers across his mouth. 'It's over, Luca.'

He turned away before she could see the tears welling in his eyes, but he was obviously not quick enough. He felt her hand on his shoulder. 'I know what you're thinking. But you're wrong.'

He blinked and turned dry-eyed back to her. 'And what am I thinking?'

'You're thinking that this is your fault. But it isn't.' She took his hands in hers and squeezed them tight. 'What happened that night was an accident, plain and simple.'

'They shouldn't have been fighting. I should have stopped them.'

'How could you? You were just a kid.'

Luca knew she was right—in his head. But in his heart he felt differently. 'I let you down.'

'How can you *say* that?' She shook her head vehemently. 'I wasn't wearing a seat belt. You saved my life when you grabbed hold of me. You never let me down. *Never.*'

Luca swallowed. He would always believe that he should have done something to change the outcome of that night, but Stefania's words went a long way to easing his guilt. Maybe in time he would be able to forgive himself.

'I don't entirely agree. But thank you.' He cleared his throat. 'I'm concerned about your sudden change of heart regarding adoption. I don't want you to rush into something you could regret later.'

'It's not sudden. I've been thinking about it for a while. I'm at peace with my decision. It feels right. In here,' she said, pressing a hand to her heart.

He opened his mouth to say something, but she held up a hand. 'No, Luca. I'm tired. Tired of trying…and failing. I'm just tired. Seven IVF attempts are more than enough. I can't take any more. Making the decision to stop riding on this merry-go-round has lifted a weight off me.'

Something—he wasn't sure what—drew his attention to the door. It was ajar. 'Do you mean that?' he asked, striding across the room and pushing the door closed.

She nodded. 'If you want to know the truth, I was ready to give up last year. I only kept going because of you and Joe.'

'What?' He tensed, muscles growing rigid. 'What are you talking about?'

She sighed. 'Even though Joe has always said having our own child wasn't that important to him, I thought he was lying just to make me feel better. But on this trip he assured me he was telling me the truth.'

'And me? Why on earth would you consider going on longer than you wanted to because of *me*? You know I only want what's best for you.'

She smiled. 'I know. But you've always blamed yourself for my inability to have children. I wanted to have a child to alleviate you of that responsibility. To ease your guilt.'

His heart palpitated, then started slamming against his ribcage as if he'd just run up ten flights of stairs. 'I can't— You can't—' He snapped his mouth closed on a ragged breath. 'I don't know what to say.'

She sighed again. 'I've tried to talk to you about the accident over the years, but whenever I brought it up you changed the subject.'

'I didn't want to hear you say you blamed me,' he admitted.

She shook her head. '*Stupido!* I never blamed you for anything. Ever. You've been the best brother a girl could want.'

Luca wasn't so sure about that. It seemed he'd made plenty of mistakes. And not just with Stefania…

The way he'd treated Morgan—was still treating her—was deplorable.

The minute Stefania left he would go to Morgan and

release her from their arrangement. He could only hope and pray that she would forgive him for misjudging her.

Because if she did not…

If she did not…

Luca didn't want to think about that. The suggestion left him gasping for breath.

CHAPTER NINE

LUCA INSERTED THE key into the lock of his Kensington apartment and pushed the door open. Now that he'd decided to tell Morgan how he felt, he couldn't wait to get on with it.

He frowned when he heard the murmur of voices coming from the lounge room. Then his face cleared. It was probably Morgan's friend Stella. Morgan had told him just last night that her friend was back from a trip to Europe and was hoping to catch up with her today.

Luca was halfway down the corridor when he realised he was wrong.

It wasn't Stella.

Or any other friend.

It was Joseph.

He knew it without even seeing him.

Knew it because he could *smell* him.

It was Joseph's expensive cologne. He recognised the scent immediately.

What was *Joseph* doing here?

Or was that a stupid question?

His heart sank down to his toes, and then rebounded into the back of his throat so fast he could hardly swallow.

He moved closer. Silently.

When he reached the doorway, he dragged in a breath and looked inside.

They were so wrapped up in each other, they didn't even notice he was there.

Luca closed his eyes, wishing the sight of them sitting so closely together on the oatmeal couch would disappear.

He opened his eyes.

They were still there.

Still talking.

Not that he'd heard a single word they said. All he could hear was the beating of his own heart, the blood thundering in his head.

Now he made a conscious effort to focus on the conversation.

'...missed you,' Morgan said, leaning towards the older man, the smile on her face the same kind of smile Luca had thought she reserved specially for him. 'It felt as if you were away for *for ever.*'

'I missed you, too,' Joseph said, holding out his hands for her to take. It was an intimate gesture. So was the way Morgan grasped his hands and squeezed them tightly. 'It wouldn't have been so bad if I'd been able to talk to you.'

'That's OK. You tried. It was great getting your message.'

Luca felt something in his chest twist tight. The phone message Morgan had just mentioned was news to him. As far as he was concerned, she had had no contact with Joseph since the call he'd intercepted. Not once had it occurred to him that Joseph would risk calling Morgan.

Ice slid through his veins. When she'd fallen apart in

his arms Morgan had been lying to him. While she'd taken him to the heights of passion she'd known about that call and said nothing.

Betrayal bit deep—until Luca almost expected wounds to miraculously appear in his flesh.

'Talking to your voicemail was hardly satisfying,' Joseph complained.

Morgan shook her head. 'I know. But I understood.'

He patted her cheek. 'I know you did. That's—' Luca's hands clenched into fists at his sides. If Joseph touched her one more time, Luca wouldn't be held responsible for his actions. 'That's one of the reasons I love you so much.'

An invisible fist hit Luca in the gut. He almost doubled over as the first wave of pain struck. It was all he could do not to gasp out loud. Another wave of agony crashed into him, almost severing him in two.

He'd heard enough. He couldn't listen to Morgan's response. Hearing her declare her love for Joseph was more than he could stand.

'Well, well, well,' he drawled, walking stiffly into the room. 'Isn't this cosy?'

Joseph jumped to his feet. Morgan, he noticed, had turned a pale shade of grey.

'What are you doing here, Joseph?' Luca demanded. 'Were you looking for me? It is my apartment, after all. Or is that a stupid question?' He barked out a harsh laugh. 'Of course it is! You'd know damned well I'd be working at this time of the day.'

'I…I…' Joseph stuttered, seemingly unable to string two successive words together. Beads of sweat formed on his upper lip and his throat.

Luca was so angry he expected steam to pour from

his ears at any moment. Cold rage filled him. He wanted to hit Joseph. Wanted to punch his lights out so badly he could taste it. If it wasn't for the fact Joseph had been ill Luca probably would have done it, too.

But that was nothing compared to what he wanted to do to Morgan.

She'd played him for a fool and he'd been stupid enough to let her.

He gave his brother-in-law a look that made the other man turn a shade of puce he'd never seen on a human face before. 'I would have thought you had more important things to do. Like signing adoption papers with your *wife!*'

Luca heard Morgan gasp, but didn't pause for long enough for either of them to answer. His patience—what little there was of it—had crashed and burned. It would take just one more word—one lie—and he was likely to do something he might live to regret.

Luca turned to Morgan with the same precision as a soldier readying to fire. 'As for you,' he said, his voice so sharp that she jumped. 'You disgust me!'

She flinched and paled until even her lips had lost colour and her hair and eyes looked blacker than black. 'You—'

Luca waved a hand through the air, cutting her off. 'Don't bother! I don't need you to draw me a map, *cara*. I heard every word. Even a blind man can see that something is going on between the two of you.' Pain filled his chest cavity but he forced himself to continue, each word like a knife slicing through him. 'You can keep your lies! It's over. It always was going to be over when Stefania came back. Just because my sister doesn't know about the two of you, it doesn't mean I was going to rub her nose in it by escorting her husband's whore around town so that everyone could laugh behind her back.'

Morgan swayed where she was sitting, and it gave Luca a savage kind of satisfaction to know that he was responsible.

'I want you out of here today.' He turned to Joseph. 'And you should be ashamed of yourself. If you ever cheat on my sister again,I'll kill you with my bare hands. Do you understand?'

Without giving either of them a chance to respond, Luca turned on his heel and stalked out of the room.

And, just like that, it was over.

'What's this all about?' Morgan asked, taking a tentative step, hands out in front of her in case she ran into something. 'You said you needed to talk to me and that it was important.'

'It is,' Morgan's best friend Stella said from a few paces ahead.

'It is,' Stella's husband Greg agreed from his position right behind her. His hands were cupped around her eyes, effectively blindfolding her. 'We're almost there.'

'There' being Greg and Stella's apartment. They'd knocked on her door a couple of minutes ago and insisted she accompany them.

'Why couldn't we talk in my place?' Morgan asked. 'Why do we have to go to yours?'

'Because.'

'Because why?'

'Just because.'

Morgan suppressed a sigh. She wasn't in the mood for this—whatever *this* was. But then she hadn't been in the mood for much of anything this past week.

Ever since Luca had—

No!

Morgan slammed a lid on her thoughts. She wouldn't think about Luca. She'd wasted enough brain cells and tears on him already. He didn't deserve any more of her time or energy.

'OK, we're here,' Greg said, his words immediately followed by the sound of the door closing, as if he'd kicked it shut with his foot. 'Are you ready, Stell?'

'Ready.'

'Keep your eyes closed until I say you can open them,' Greg instructed, loosening his hands.

Morgan stood there, dutifully doing as she was told.

'OK, you can open them.'

She opened her eyes and blinked against the bright lights.

'Surprise!' Stella and Greg said in unison.

Her heart did a stutter step then took off at a gallop. 'What is all this? Why are you wearing those goofy hats?'

Both were wearing pointed foil party hats embossed with multicoloured balloons. The coffee table was laden with a scrumptious-looking cheese platter, little bowls of dips and olives, and a bottle of champagne on ice.

'We want to help you celebrate your new job,' Greg said. 'We also thought you could do with cheeri— Hey! What did you do that for?' he asked, as Stella dug an elbow into his ribs.

Stella rolled her eyes before passing Morgan a hat. 'Here, put this on.'

As she took the hat and slipped the elastic cord under her chin, Morgan felt tears sting the backs of her eyes. 'You didn't have to go to all this trouble!'

'Of course we did. We're your best friends. Who else would you celebrate with?'

Who indeed? Morgan thought.

A week ago she would have celebrated with Luca. He would have—

Damn it! She was doing it again. Thinking about Luca when she'd promised herself she wouldn't.

'Come on, Greg.' Stella was practically bouncing up and down with excitement. 'Open up the champagne.'

Morgan didn't feel like celebrating. Yes, she was pleased she'd finally secured a job—even if it wasn't as good as her position at Enigma Marketing.

Life could return to normal.

Only it didn't feel normal.

Her old life didn't feel right any more.

What was once familiar now felt alien.

It was as if her existence could be separated into two parts. Before Luca...and after Luca.

Morgan smothered a groan. Luca again. Why couldn't she get the dratted man out of her head?

'Earth to Morgan, earth to Morgan. Are you in there?'

Her head shot up. 'What?'

Greg waved a glass of champagne under her nose. 'I'm waiting for you to take this so that we can make a toast.'

Morgan plastered a bright smile on her face. She didn't want to be a wet blanket. If she wasn't in cele-bratory mode that was her problem. For her friends' sake, she had to make an effort and pretend that she was.

Over the next hour, she did exactly that. She drank champagne and she ate cheese. She tried Stella's famous smoked salmon dip and raved about her roast capsicum relish.

And she drank more champagne.

She smiled. And she smiled. She smiled until her cheeks felt as if they were about to crack.

And she laughed. Laughed until she almost cried.

She thought she'd done a pretty good job of pretending that she was having a good time—until Greg deposited a premium box of Da Silva Chocolate in front of her.

'Dessert,' he said with a flourish.

Morgan stared at the box as if it was a cobra dancing in the centre of the coffee table. Her face froze, her insides going rigid. Barely able to breathe, she put a hand protectively out in front of her. 'Take them away.'

'But they're your favourites.'

'I don't care. Take them away.'

Greg took one look at her face and did as she asked.

As soon as they were alone, Stella sat forward on the couch. 'OK—spill.'

Morgan dragged her gaze away from the chocolates. 'What?'

'Tell me what's going on.'

'With what?'

Stella rolled her eyes. 'What do you think? With Luca da Silva, of course.'

Morgan flinched. 'There's nothing to tell.'

'Oh, yes, there is. I mention the man's name and you look like you've sucked on a lemon. You see a box of his chocolates and, instead of jumping on them the way you usually do, you look as if Greg has handed you a spider or something equally nasty. Why is that?'

How could she explain that hearing Luca's name hurt? How could she explain that she would never be able to look at a box of chocolates again without remembering the tender way Luca had made love to her?

'You're exaggerating.'

Stella shook her head vigorously. 'No, I'm not. You walk around like a ghost half the time. And while you've done a good imitation of looking like someone who's happy in the last hour or so, you haven't fooled anyone. Now, I've kept quiet and haven't asked any questions, because that's the way you've wanted it. But I'm not going to keep quiet any more. What did that man do to you?'

'I don't know what you're talking about. Luca—' She dragged in a breath. It hurt to say his name. 'He didn't do anything to me.'

'Come on, Morgan,' Stella said gently. 'We've been friends far too long for you to pull the wool over my eyes.'

'I'm not.'

'Yes, you are,' Greg said, as he walked into the room and sat down beside his wife. 'There's something odd about the whole situation. One day you're spitting chips because the guy has had you fired, and the next day you're going out with him as if nothing has happened.'

'*And* you moved in with him after only knowing him for a matter of days,' Stella said. 'That's not like you at all.'

'No, it's not,' Greg said emphatically.

'And then, barely two weeks later, you move back into your apartment and start walking around as if somebody has died.' Stella folded her arms. 'You're not going anywhere until you tell us exactly what's going on.'

Morgan tried to stare them both down. But with two against one—and a couple of glasses of champagne under her belt—it was an unequal battle. Finally, she sighed, 'OK. You win.'

Briefly and concisely, and as unemotionally as she could, Morgan gave them a step-by-step account of the last month.

When she told them how Luca had blackmailed her into becoming his mistress, Greg jumped to his feet and said, 'I'll kill the bastard.'

They listened intently as she recounted what had happened during that last awful scene, when Luca had found her and Joseph together.

When she had finished they sat in silence for quite a long time, before Stella whistled through her teeth. 'I bet Joseph made mincemeat out of Luca.'

Morgan shook her head. 'He didn't get a chance. Luca walked out before either of us could get a word in edgeways, and he flew to the US that same day.'

Stella rolled her eyes. 'There are telephones.'

Morgan sighed. 'If you must know, I asked Joseph not to say anything.'

'Why the hell not? And, come to think of it, why are you so damned miserable? I'd have thought you'd be jumping for joy. Your father knows everything. Luca can't hold it over your head any more. His blackmail is over and done with. You're free. Isn't that what you wanted?'

Morgan dragged in a deep breath that did nothing to ease the empty, bottomless void inside her and slowly shook her head.

'I don't understand,' Stella said, clearly confused.

'I did something really stupid,' Morgan whispered.

Stella and Greg exchanged puzzled glances before Stella asked quietly, 'What did you do?'

Morgan's composure, which she'd built around herself like a fortress, began to crack and crumble. Tears filled her eyes and emotion clogged her throat as she croaked miserably, 'I fell in love with him.'

Stella's eyes widened. 'Oh, you poor thing! That explains everything.'

'Luca, are you listening to me?'

Luca's head shot up, his eyes focussing on the face of the woman sitting opposite. Kristy—or was it Kathy?—was beautiful. Very beautiful. He'd met her at a party the last time he was in New York, and had promised to call her the next time he was in town.

He'd waited until he'd wrapped up his business—which had only taken him a week when it should have taken at least two. He'd worked everyone around him hard, and he'd worked himself even harder.

But even though he'd fallen exhausted into bed every night, it hadn't stopped the dreams.

Every night he dreamt about her.

Tormenting dreams that—

'*Luca!* Did you hear what I said?' the blonde asked with a pout.

He hadn't.

Not a single word.

He was doing what he'd promised himself he would not do.

Thinking about Morgan.

About how she tasted when he kissed her.

And how she looked when he was deep inside her.

'*Luca!*'

The pout turned into a full-on glower. Luca realised that sitting opposite her was the last place he wanted to be. 'I'm sorry,' he said. 'But I have to go.'

She gazed at him as if he'd lost him mind, and Luca

wondered if indeed he had. He tossed some money onto
the table to pay for the meal that was yet to be served
to them, escorted Kathy or Kristy or whatever her name
was into a taxi, and then flagged Gino over.

'Where to, boss?'

'Take me back to my apartment.' He had apartments
in several major cities around the world, including New
York. 'Be ready to leave first thing in the morning.'

'We're going home?'

Luca tapped his thigh. In theory he should return to
London. It was the principal base of his operations and
he had meetings scheduled.

But he wasn't ready to return home just yet.

He refused to think about exactly why that was—
and certainly wouldn't accept that it had anything to
do with Morgan.

'No. If I can get Tad Okimura to bring forward our
meeting, we'll go to Japan.'

The following morning Luca had just boarded his
private jet for the flight—Mr Okimura had willingly
agreed to an earlier meeting—when Gino tapped him
on the shoulder. 'Luca, I think you should take a look
at this before we take off.'

Eager to be on his way, Luca was about to dismiss
the suggestion when he saw the look on Gino's face.
'What is it?' he asked, holding out his hand.

'This morning's paper.'

Luca took one look at the tabloid and froze.
Da Silva Adoption,' the headline screamed. It didn't
matter that Stefania's surname was really Langdon.
She was part of the da Silva family and the da Silva
family was news.

Quickly, he scanned the article. His scalp crawled

when the column mentioned the seven failed IVF attempts and went on to reveal their recent decision to adopt.

The journalist kept quoting 'a confidential source'.

There was only one person Luca could think of who was privy to that level of information and whom he didn't trust as far as he could throw her.

Morgan.

He'd made the mistake of mentioning the adoption in front of her the previous week. Maybe this was her idea of payback. Or maybe it was her way of forcing Joseph's hand. If that was the case then she was in for one hell of a big surprise—because, despite his declaration of love to Morgan, Joseph also loved his wife, and Luca was convinced he would never willingly leave her.

Icy anger slithered serpent-like inside him. He'd warned Morgan what would happen if she did this. Promised her that if she harmed Stefania in any way she would regret the day she'd ever met him.

It was a promise he was looking forward to keeping!

His fingers closed around the paper so fiercely it ripped in several places. Luca looked at his security chief. 'Tell the pilot we're returning to London.'

Gino nodded and headed to the cockpit.

Luca gritted his teeth. She would pay for this. He would make sure of it.

With every kilometre the plane flew Luca's anger increased. By the time the plane taxied to the terminal in London he was practically jumping out of his skin.

As soon as he was in the waiting car, Luca dialled Morgan's phone. There was no answer, so he left a message for her to call him.

Then he waited.

* * *

When Morgan turned on her phone, there were two messages waiting for her.

The first message was from Luca. As soon as she heard his voice, she almost keeled over. If she hadn't already been sitting down, she'd have fallen down.

'Morgan. It's Luca. Call me as soon as you get this message.'

Morgan frowned, dragged in a breath, and then pressed the requisite button to replay the message. His accent was thick, as it always was when he was angry or aroused. Given that his speech was also clipped, as if he'd been speaking through clenched teeth, she guessed it was the former.

The second call was from Stella. The content of her call was disturbing. 'What's going on, Morgan? Have you seen the article about Stefania and Joseph in the paper? Call me.'

Paper? Article? What on earth was Stella talking about?

Morgan hadn't seen a paper this morning. This was only her second day at her new job and she was trying to make a good impression.

She hurried out of her office to Reception, where she knew they kept a stack of papers. She quickly flipped through and discarded several before finding the article in one of the tabloids.

'Oh, no!'

She put a hand to her mouth.

How could this have happened?

Who would do such a terrible thing?

Suddenly her heart stilled, the breath locking tight in her lungs.

So that was why Luca was looking for her.

She didn't need anyone to draw her a picture.

Luca thought *she'd* done this.

Well, he was wrong.

He was wrong about a lot of things.

And it was about time she told him so!

It was hours—four, to be precise—before Morgan finally returned Luca's call. By then he was so taut with anger and frustration that he didn't know what to do with himself.

He'd had Gino driving around and around in circles and the looks his security chief kept giving him in the rear vision mirror suggested he thought Luca had lost his mind.

When the phone rang, it took him all of two seconds to snatch it off the seat beside him. 'Where the hell have you been?' he gritted from between tightly clenched teeth.

'Busy,' she said, in a sweet tone that immediately made his hands clench into fists. 'At my new job.'

Luca ignored that. 'Where are you?'

'Ah, now that's an interesting question.'

The tone of her voice immediately made his stomach muscles contract into a mass of tight knots. 'What does that mean?'

'It means I've just had afternoon tea with Joseph and Stefania,' Morgan said softly. 'Your sister is a lovely woman. As to where I am, well, I'm right here in their sitting room.'

Luca was still trying to absorb her words when the phone went dead. Shock reverberated through his system in waves, his body stiffening until it felt as if he'd been spray-painted with quick-drying cement.

Dio! He would have her head for this!

'Gino. My sister's house. And make it fast.'

Putting the phone back to his ear, he pressed the speed dial number for Morgan's phone, but it went immediately to her voicemail. Cursing under his breath in both Italian and English, he disconnected without leaving a message.

'Can't you go any faster?' he demanded.

'I'm going as fast as I can, boss.'

Luca flung himself back against the seat and for the rest of the journey sat with his teeth clenched and his hands braced against his thighs.

When they finally reached Stefania's Knightsbridge home, Luca leapt from the vehicle before it had even stopped moving. He marched up the steps to the front door, where he pressed the doorbell with one hand while using the other to pound the ornate brass knocker against its matching panel.

A maid opened the door. Luca brushed past her. 'Where is she?'

'Your sister has stepped out for a short while,' the maid replied nervously.

'Not her. Morgan. Ms Marshall.' Luca could barely force the words out through numb lips.

'Oh, Ms Marshall. She's waiting for you in the sitting room. Would you like me to bring through some refreshments?'

'No, we won't be needing any.' They might need a body bag by the time he'd finished with her, though. He felt as if he'd left the civilised part of him behind somewhere.

Striding through the foyer, Luca threw open the double doors by thumping them forcefully with his palms. His eyes scanned the room, coming to rest on the slender form of Morgan, standing by the window.

For a moment all he could do was stare.

She was dressed in the same outfit she'd been wearing the day he'd met her...including his favourite I'm-in-charge black leather boots.

Two nights before he'd found her with Joseph, Luca had finally lived out his fantasy of making love to her while she was wearing nothing else but those boots. When he'd told her to leave them on, she'd blushed. At the time he'd seen her reaction as evidence of her inexperience, but he'd obviously just been fooling himself.

He crossed the room with a speed that would have surprised him had he had time to think about it. His hand went to her throat, where he applied just enough pressure to back her up against the window ledge.

He put his face close to hers and bared his teeth. 'I told you what would happen if you hurt my sister.'

'I didn't—'

Luca wasn't listening. He was a man possessed.

If Morgan had been a man she would already be lying prostrate on the floor, knocked there by the series of blows Luca would have thrown. Because she was a woman, he did the next best thing.

He dropped his head and fused his mouth with hers. He kissed her savagely, driven by the need to hurt. He forced her lips apart when she clamped her mouth closed. He gripped the tops of her arms in a vice-like grip when she struggled against him.

And all the while her betrayal tormented him like swords of ice-cold steel digging into his flesh.

Suddenly the stiletto heel of her boot landed on his left foot.

Luca sprang backwards. He hopped onto his good

foot, shaking the other one in the air, hoping the throbbing would dissipate.

It was then, while he was teetering on one foot, that she struck. Moving so quickly she was nothing more than a flash of movement, Morgan quickly put her left foot behind his right ankle and pushed—hard.

Surprise and momentum sent Luca tumbling to the floor. Keeping his wits about him, he grabbed a handful of Morgan's jacket at the last moment and pulled her down with him.

Luca landed on his back on the carpet with Morgan sprawled on top of him. She pushed her hair back off her face and glared at him, black eyes glittering. 'Let me go!'

'No.'

She planted her hands on the carpet on either side of him and braced her body to push herself away from him.

Acting quickly, Luca rolled over, reversing their positions.

'Let me go, you…you jerk,' she said, struggling harder.

Luca gasped as her elbow connected forcefully with his ribcage. She was wriggling like an eel, her arms and legs whipping around like a windmill gone crazy. A knee just missed his groin.

Adjusting their position, Luca pinned her more securely, capturing her arms and legs against her sides. When she was lying quiescent beneath him, Luca asked again, 'What did you do that for?'

'You were hurting me, damn it!'

Luca froze.

He'd rushed over here crazed with anger. Mad with rage. He'd wanted to lash out at her for hurting Stefania. But now that he was here—now that he'd seen her again and had tasted her again—Luca realised his wild behaviour had very little to do with his sister and everything to do with him.

He'd thought he'd found the one woman he could trust, and she'd taken his heart and smashed it into a million pieces.

The realisation gutted him, and it was all he could do not to howl with pain.

He'd wanted to hurt her as she'd hurt him.

Emotionally...not physically.

Her words had brought him crashing back to reality.

Dragging in a breath, he felt a small measure of sanity return. 'I'm sorry,' he said roughly.

She didn't answer him.

With carefully controlled movements, he rolled off her and rose to his feet. He held out his hand for her to take but she ignored it, scrambling to her feet without his assistance.

Luca stared at her as she tucked her blouse into her skirt and smoothed her hands—shaking hands, he noted—down over her slender hips.

'Why, Morgan?' he asked hoarsely. 'Why did you come here?'

'Because it was time the truth was told,' Morgan said calmly.

Luca inhaled sharply. Ice slid down his spine. He couldn't comprehend that Morgan had just said what she'd said to him. Couldn't grasp that the woman who had looked at him so tenderly as she melted in his arms could so coolly and calmly tell him she'd just destroyed his sister's life.

'I— You—' Luca snapped his mouth closed, too stunned to know what to say.

And then the anger came.

Waves of it, smashing into him, stealing his breath and sending his blood roaring through his veins.

He rushed at her, pinning her up against the window ledge again. 'I could kill you for this. I warned you what would happen if you hurt Stefania!'

'But I haven't hurt Stefania.'

She sounded so calm Luca wanted to shake her until her teeth rattled. Instead, he gripped her even tighter. 'Do you really think she is thrilled to see her private agony spilled across the pages of the tabloids for the world to read? Is that what you think?' he demanded, dealing with the lesser of two evils first. He couldn't bring himself to imagine how Stefania had reacted to the news that Joseph and Morgan were having an affair.

She tossed her head. Her black hair swirled around her shoulders and sent an invisible cloud of orange scent into the air. 'Is that an accusation, Luca?' she asked quietly.

CHAPTER TEN

LUCA STARED AT her and kept on staring.

Morgan stared right back, black eyes glinting with challenge, head tilted back with angry pride.

He'd seen that look about her before. More than once.

Now, as then, he found it difficult to look at her and believe she'd done the things she'd done. But he'd seen her with his very own eyes. Heard her with his very own ears.

His anger evaporated, exposing the raw pain underneath. 'I don't know what it is,' he said wearily. 'I don't know what to think.'

A shadow flickered across her face. 'Don't you?'

She looked sad. Disappointed. Hurt.

Luca wanted to believe the emotions etched on her face were genuine, but Morgan had lied to his face more than once—and looked like an innocent angel as she did so.

'No. No, I don't.' He raked a hand through his hair and around the back of his neck. 'I want to believe you had nothing to do with the leak to the papers, but who else could have told them?'

Her eyes flashed fire at him again. 'Any number of people, I'd have thought.'

'Like who?'

'What about someone at the IVF clinic? Or the adoption agency? What about one of the staff who work here in this very house? Maybe they saw a way to earn a bit of extra cash on the side? Who knows? I can think of a dozen possibilities.' She stabbed him in the centre of the chest with the tip of her finger. 'But you can't even bring yourself to give me the benefit of the doubt, can you?'

Luca remained silent, staring at her, his heart sitting at the back of his throat.

Her reaction bothered him.

It was one thing to deny the charge, but quite another to challenge him outright the way Morgan was doing.

'Can you?' she shouted.

Luca stared at her. His chest felt so tight he could hardly breathe.

Images rushed through his mind at kaleidoscopic speed.

He saw again the look on her face as she'd tossed his cheque back in his face.

Saw her marching away from him, spine rigid and shoulders squared, angry pride radiating from her in waves.

Saw the brightly defiant gleam in her eyes every time he pushed and she shoved straight back.

Saw her eyes widen as he entered her, and again when she climaxed.

Luca exhaled slowly, the truth filtering through his bloodstream.

He'd done it again. Let his emotions rule his head so that he couldn't think straight.

He stared deeply into her eyes. 'Yes. In fact, I can do

better than just giving you the benefit of the doubt. I can say outright that you had nothing to do with the article. You wouldn't do something like that.'

'You see. You—' She stopped, gasped, then said slowly, 'Say that again.'

'I believe you. You didn't leak the information to the papers.'

She seemed to sag before his eyes, as if the fire inside her had suddenly been extinguished. Then her eyes filled with tears.

His heart wrenching, Luca reached for her. But when he tried to pull her closer she resisted.

Luca had never felt so helpless. Or so unsure of himself. 'Hush, *cara*. Don't cry. I'm sorry. So, so sorry.'

She sniffed, dragged in a breath, and then exhaled slowly. She stared him straight in the eye and said calmly, 'The leak to the newspaper came from Da Silva Chocolate.'

Luca felt winded, as if an invisible fist had punched him in the stomach. Every word she'd just uttered rebounded inside his head, as if someone had taken a hammer and was beating on the inside of his skull.

'What—? Who—? I don't understand.'

'Do you believe me?' she demanded.

Luca didn't hesitate. 'Yes, I believe you.'

Her chin angled into the air, a glint of challenge in her eyes. 'Are you sure?'

He nodded. 'I'm sure.'

'Because if you're not, you can always check with your sister when she gets back.'

Luca knew better than to doubt her again. 'That won't be necessary.'

She looked pleased by his response.

His gaze sharpened, her words finally penetrating. 'Stefania knows about this?'

Morgan nodded. 'Yes. She's the one who told me.'

Luca gasped. 'How does *she* know where the leak came from?'

'Joseph pulled some strings and set up a meeting with the journalist. Stefania promised him an interview if he revealed the name of his source.'

'Who was it…?'

He held his breath as he waited for her to answer. Whoever was responsible would learn what a terrible mistake they'd made crossing his family. He did not make a good enemy; he would ensure they were punished for what they'd done.

'Can't you guess?' she asked, her eyes locked steadily on his.

His scalp crawled and a wave of unease slid serpent-like down his spine. 'Olivia. It was Olivia, wasn't it?'

Morgan nodded.

Fury rose up inside him like a two-headed monster. Unable to stand still, Luca began pacing the floor. *'Madre del Dio!* She will pay for this.'

Suddenly he ground to a halt and spun to face Morgan, his hands clamped into fists at his side, a frown on his face. 'But how did she find out about the IVF treatments and their plan to adopt?'

Even as the words left his mouth he knew. His meeting with Stefania the day she'd arrived back from Australia replayed through his mind. He saw again the moment when he'd suddenly noticed the door was ajar.

Had a hint of movement or a barely audible sound drawn his attention to the doorway? Something certainly had. Only he'd been so engrossed in his conversation with Stefania it hadn't registered at the time.

His teeth gritted. 'The door. She was listening at the damned door!'

'It wouldn't surprise me. She's one ambitious woman. I wouldn't put anything past her.'

Neither would he, Luca acknowledged. A woman capable of leaking personal information to the press— for money, revenge or whatever twisted motive she'd had—was capable of anything.

'You'll also be pleased to know Stefania isn't upset by the article,' Morgan continued.

'She's not?'

Morgan shook her head. 'No, she's not. She was to start with, but then she realised she had something to offer other women in the same situation.'

'Meaning?'

'She's hoping that by giving an in depth interview, she can help other women make the decision to adopt.'

'I see.'

How had he got things so wrong? Luca asked himself.

And then he realised the answer was standing right in front of him.

Morgan.

Luca raked a hand through his hair and around the back of his neck, tension clawing at his insides. Stefania had called him stupid more than once, and that was exactly what he was. Stupid. He'd been acting that way from the moment Morgan had walked into his office in those I'm-in-charge black boots, with her hair swirling around her shoulders and her black eyes blazing.

And the day he'd found her with Joseph was his crowning glory!

Because without even hearing what Morgan had to say about the scene he'd interrupted, he knew he was wrong about that, too. At least about Morgan's role in it.

The woman who had whispered his name as she'd fallen apart in his arms would never betray him.

The woman who had kissed him as if she wanted to be with him for ever would not lie.

Morgan had tried to tell him that, but he'd been too upset to listen.

He just hoped he wasn't too late to undo the damage.

He dragged in a deep breath. 'I'm sorry about last week, *cara*.'

He heard her breath catch. 'Are you? Are you really?'

There was no mistaking the pain in her voice and his heart wrenched. 'I am. What can I do to make it up to you?'

'Nothing. It's too late for that.'

Pain pierced his heart. 'Don't say that,' he said roughly, his insides twisting into a knot. His arms wrapped around her. 'It's not too late. It can't be.'

She pushed against his chest. 'Let me go, Luca.'

He shook his head. 'No. Never. You're mine now. I'm never going to let you go.'

Her eyes flickered with an emotion he couldn't define. 'That's not your decision to make.'

'If you just let me explain—'

She tore herself away from him. 'Like you let *me* explain last week?'

'I know. I was a fool. I was upset.'

She shook her head. 'You weren't upset. You were angry.'

'True. But with men, one usually follows the other.'

'Maybe.' She stared into his face for a long time

and then sighed. 'If it's any consolation I understand
why you found it so difficult to believe I was telling
the truth.'

'You do?'

She nodded. 'The accident made you feel so over-
protective of Stefania you weren't able to see the wood
for the trees. And I guess having a mother who cheated
on your father didn't help.'

He shook his head. 'No, it didn't. I was determined
not to follow in my father's footsteps.'

'I can understand that.'

He took a step closer. 'Does that mean you forgive
me?'

She stared steadily back at him, then bit down on her
lower lip. 'I can forgive you for thinking badly about me
in the beginning. I might have done the same thing in
the circumstances. But what I can't forgive is the way
you turned on me last week.'

Luca's heart sank, a sick feeling clutching at the back
of his throat. He grasped her shoulders. 'Do you think
I'm not kicking myself for that? But you have to understand what it looked like. Finding the two of you
together, hearing him say he loved you, was a shock.'
For a minute he couldn't go on, remembered pain
stabbing at his insides. 'I was too hurt to listen to reason.'

Morgan wanted to believe him. Wanted to believe the
hoarseness of his voice was the result of pain.

But she couldn't.

She clasped her hands tightly together in front of
her. 'You should know me better by now. You should
have given me a chance to explain.'

'Yes, I should have. I'm sorry, *cara*.' His fingers

tightened on her shoulders. 'Believe me. I will never make the same mistake again.'

Could she trust him? She wanted to—so badly she could taste it. But every time she let herself believe they had a future together something happened to show her she was fooling herself.

Luca had broken her heart. She couldn't take it happening again. She opened her mouth to tell him that it was over, but quickly shut it again.

She had a habit of speaking first and thinking second.

Only this time the stakes were far too high for her to reject Luca outright. If there was a chance he was telling her the truth then she would grasp it with both hands and never let go.

'You haven't asked me what I'm doing here,' she said slowly.

He smiled. 'And I don't intend to. Whatever your reasons, your motives are honourable. You didn't come here to cause trouble or to harm anyone.'

She searched his face. He met her gaze steadily and she felt hope bloom to life inside of her.

If Luca had demanded an explanation she would have given him one. But the fact that he had faith in her without one meant a lot to her.

Still, it wasn't enough.

Much as she wanted to fling herself into his arms and tell him she forgave him, there was still the matter of Joseph to deal with.

That…and Luca's decision to blackmail her.

She folded her arms. 'What about Joseph?'

The question lingered in the air. The room suddenly seemed very still. Very quiet. So much so Morgan imagined she could hear her heart beating.

'What about him?' Luca asked. His voice had an edge to it and his facial muscles had tightened imperceptibly.

'Do you believe we're just friends?' she asked, tension reknotting her shoulders until it felt as though she was carrying a heavy weight on them.

Luca hesitated for a fraction of a second. 'I believe you see him as just a friend.'

Her insides stiffened. Luca's hesitation had been a fraction too long. And his answer was only a part answer. 'That isn't what I asked. Are you going to accept Joseph as my friend?'

Luca stiffened. She watched it happen. 'No. No, I'm not.'

'Why?'

'Because I don't think Joseph's motives in wanting your friendship are as innocent as yours. Don't forget I saw the two of you together. I saw the way he touched you. They were not the actions of a man only interested in friendship. His feelings run a lot deeper than that.'

Morgan frowned. Luca had a point. Joseph's feelings *were* a lot deeper than mere friendship. Luca's instincts were right about that. He just hadn't realised it was paternal love he had seen rather than the love a man felt for a woman.

Was that his fault?

No. It wasn't.

But…

And it was a big but…

She unfolded her arms and clenched her hands into fists at her sides. 'You're missing the point.'

'Am I? Then perhaps you'd better explain it to me.'

'Oh, I intend to. Don't worry about that.' She stabbed him in the middle of his chest with the tip of her finger.

'How can you say you believe me when you don't trust my judgement?'

'I think you are innocent in the ways of men. We are far more basic creatures than you might think. Friendship with women is not high on our agenda.'

Morgan snorted. 'Tell me something I don't know. I sometimes think sex is all you men think about!'

He smiled. 'I rest my case.'

Morgan stamped her foot. 'I know when a man is attracted to me, damn it, and Joseph isn't!'

Suddenly the door behind them sprang open. Joseph and Stefania were framed in the doorway.

Joseph was wearing a heavy frown. 'What the hell is going on in here? We could hear you arguing all the way from the front door!'

Luca froze until his entire body was rigid. The last thing he needed right at this moment was to be confronted by Joseph.

'You keep out of this. You've caused enough trouble,' he snapped, unable to contain his frustration.

'Luca!'

He wasn't sure who had spoken first. Stefania or Morgan. Both were glowering at him.

Luca looked from one face to another. What was it about Joseph Langdon that inspired these women to spring to his defence?

He could understand his sister wanting to protect her husband. That was what a wife should do.

But what about Morgan?

If she and Joseph were just friends then she should put *him*—Luca da Silva—first.

Not second.

Not third.

But first, damn it!

'Don't worry, ladies,' Joseph said, sauntering into the room, his wife hot on his heels. 'I think it's time Luca and I had a showdown.'

'Now, Joe, don't forget you've been ill. I—'

Joseph held up a hand. 'No, Stef. I'm not going to be quiet. Not this time.' He stared Luca in the eye, his expression harder than Luca had ever seen. 'Morgan and I had a long conversation after you left us last week. She filled me in on what happened while I was away.'

Ice slid down Luca's spine. 'All of it?'

Joseph nodded. 'All of it.'

Luca spared Stefania the briefest of glances. Her face gave nothing away.

Did she know what they were talking about?

He hoped the hell that she did not.

He turned back to Joseph. 'And how does it make you feel knowing that Morgan has found pleasure in my bed?'

Luca heard Morgan gasp, but kept his eyes trained on his brother-in-law.

Joseph surged towards him. Stefania grabbed his arm and forced him to a halt several feet away. 'It makes me ill. But not for the reason you think, you bastard! I ought to punch your lights out for blackmailing the poor girl into sleeping with you.'

'Joe—don't,' Stefania pleaded beside him.

'I won't let this go, Stef. I can't. Morgan is too important to me.'

Joseph's words bounced off the inside of Luca's skull.

He closed his eyes.

He felt sick.

Sick to the stomach.

Sick to his very soul.

He would never have imagined this scene would be played out in front of Stefania. He'd tried so hard to avoid this very situation. So hard to protect her. But all his plans lay in dust at his feet.

Slowly, he opened his eyes.

He didn't look at Stefania.

He couldn't.

Couldn't look at the pain on her face and in her eyes after hearing her husband pledge his feelings for another woman for all to hear.

His eyes focussed on Joseph's face, and the anger that had been simmering for months boiled over.

Without thinking, Luca stormed across the distance separating them and hauled Joseph to the tips of his toes by the lapels of his blue blazer. 'I could kill you for hurting Stefania like this.'

He heard Morgan and Stefania gasp, but ignored them both.

So, too, did Joseph, who bared his teeth in a near snarl. 'You have gall—do you know that? What have I ever done to make you think I would hurt Steph? I love her, you fool.'

Luca stared at him and kept on staring.

'Look at her,' Joseph urged harshly. 'Go on. Look at her.'

Luca stared at Joseph for a long moment. Then he turned his head slowly, as if he was moving in slow motion, and looked at Stefania. His heart was sitting at the back of his throat in fear of what he might find.

He raked his gaze over Stefania's face. She stared back at him with wide, pleading eyes. Eyes that showed concern but no obvious signs of distress.

Confusion washed over him in waves.

Slowly he let go of Joseph's lapels and took a step backwards. 'Sorry,' he muttered.

Joseph straightened his jacket. 'Don't worry about it. In your position I'd probably have done the same. And besides, it warms my heart to know that if anything ever happened to me you'd be here to look after Stef for me.'

His wife hugged his arm. 'Nothing is going to happen to you. I won't allow it.'

Luca watched them. There was true affection between them. A bond of love he'd been blind to for the last few months.

He should have known Joseph wouldn't betray the wife he adored.

He looked from Stefania to Joseph and back again.

Then he looked at Morgan.

She was staring at him as if he'd grown two heads, her hands clasped tightly together in front of her.

Anxiety tugged at the base of his spine. Then tugged some more.

'Who is Morgan to you?' he demanded, turning back to Joseph. 'Tell me what she means to you.'

Joseph met his eyes steadily. 'Morgan is my daughter.'

The surprise was so great Luca reeled backwards, his breath jagging in the back of his throat like a serrated knife. 'Your what...?'

'My daughter.'

Hearing it a second time didn't make it any easier to swallow.

While he was still reeling, Joseph briefly and con- cisely explained.

The story was a typical one. Joseph had been in his last year at Oxford University when he'd met a local girl waitressing in a pub where the students hung out. One night he'd had too much to drink and the two of them had slept together.

It had never happened again.

He'd finished his degree and moved back to London, where his fiancée had been waiting for him, not once suspecting that he was leaving behind a woman pregnant with his child.

Luca barely absorbed the details; he was still in shock.

He thought about the accusations he'd thrown and gritted his teeth.

He thought about everything he'd done and clenched his hands into fists.

And then he thought about those times in the middle of the night when he'd lain awake, unable to sleep, because of thoughts of Joseph and Morgan together.

And she hadn't said a word.

Not a damned word.

Fury crackled up his spine.

'I believe I owe you an apology,' he said stiffly, holding out his hand.

Joseph looked from his hand to his face and back again. Then he angled his chin into the air in the exact same way Morgan had done so many times without Luca once realising why the action was so familiar.

'I believe you do.' Joseph reached out and clasped his hand, squeezing tight. 'But I'm not the only person you need to apologise to.'

Luca followed Joseph's glance at Morgan. 'If you'd give us a few moments alone, then I'd be happy to give Morgan everything she deserves,' he said, with an outward show of calm he was far from feeling inside.

Joseph stared at him with narrowed eyes. 'Morgan

kept our secret at great cost to herself—something I will always be grateful for. Do I have your word you will treat her with respect?'

Luca nodded. 'You do.'

Joseph looked at his daughter. 'Morgan…?'

'I'll be fine.'

'In that case, we'll leave you to it.'

He took hold of Stefania's hand, but she obviously wasn't ready to leave just yet. 'Wait.' She extracted her hand from her husband's and walked across to Luca. 'I want you to know that I am OK with this. More than OK. I have already welcomed Morgan into the family and will be honoured to be her stepmother. So there is no need for you to go looking for revenge or anything stupid like that.'

'How long have you known?' he asked.

'Joe confessed while we were in Australia.'

'I see.' Luca remembered Stefania's mysterious comment about discussing something with Joseph that had happened a long time ago and which she was unable to tell him about yet.

No doubt Joseph's secret daughter was what she'd been referring to.

'The strain of keeping their secret was what landed him in hospital in the first place. He realised he couldn't keep quiet any longer. But, had he not, Morgan would have forced his hand.' She touched his hand and smiled. 'Perhaps you should ask her why.'

As soon as the door closed behind them, Luca turned towards Morgan.

She took one look at his face and began backing away from him. She held up her hand. 'Don't, Luca.'

Luca followed her retreat. 'Don't what?'

'Don't come any closer or I'll use another of Gino's moves on you. Only this time you won't get off so easily.'

'So that's where you learnt that little manoeuvre from, is it? I'm going to have to have a word with Gino about that.' Her back came up against the windowsill. He stopped inches from her. 'You have some explaining to do. You lied to me.'

She tossed her head, sending an invisible cloud of her fragrance into the air. 'You deserved to be lied to.'

'Is that so?' he asked silkily.

'Yes, it is. You had no right to come after me the way you did. It was wrong. You should have spoken to Joseph, not me. You should have threatened to punch his lights out if you thought he was cheating on Stefania.'

Luca inclined his head. 'You're right. I should have. Just as you should have told me the truth.'

'I couldn't. I'd promised Joseph I wouldn't tell anyone. He was terrified of losing Stefania. She was so upset about her inability to conceive. She felt like a failure as a wife. And as a woman. He felt he couldn't present her with a child from a previous relationship at a time like that.'

'Perhaps. But by protecting Stefania, Joseph betrayed you. Have you thought about that?' He paused for a moment, and then added softly, 'Just as you, by protecting Joseph, betrayed me.'

'I didn't betray you,' she protested.

'No?' He tunnelled a hand under her hair and pulled her towards him, then bent his head and feathered a kiss against the corner of her mouth. 'You lay in my arms, let me make love to you, and all the while these pretty lips were lying to me. What is that if not betrayal?'

'I…I…'

'Well…?'

She tossed her head again. 'I had no choice.'

This time the fury riding his spine hissed and sizzled. He cupped her throat. 'You *had* a choice. You chose to lie to me. As little as ten minutes ago you were still lying to me. I had to hear the truth from someone else.'

'He's my father, Luca.'

'And I am your lover!' Luca roared, eyes searing into hers. 'I am the man you should put above all others.'

He felt her swallow against his palm. 'That's only because…only because…'

'Only because what…?'

'You blackmailed me.'

Luca stiffened. He'd always thought of angry emotions as being red. But he was wrong about that. They were black. Such a deep, intense black he was almost blinded by them.

The hand cupping her throat moved until his fingers were pressed against her mouth. 'Do not *dare* suggest the only reason we were lovers is because I blackmailed you. That might be the way it started, but it is not the way it ended—is it?'

Slowly she shook her head. 'No. No, it's not.'

'You want to be with me, don't you?'

'Yes,' she whispered.

Satisfaction raced through him.

But it wasn't enough.

Not nearly enough.

'You want to be with me more than life itself?'

'Yes.'

Luca swooped on her mouth, kissing her until they were both breathing heavily. He lifted his head. 'So our

scoreboard is even, is it not?' he asked, his accent and
his voice both thickening. 'I forgive you for lying to me
and you forgive me for blackmailing you. *Si?*'

'I don't think—'

Luca kissed the words right out of her mouth. His
kiss was tender. Sweet. Heart pounding, he lifted his
head and looked deep into her eyes. *'Si?'*

'Si…' she breathed, collapsing against his chest.

Luca slid his arms around her waist, pulling her closer
so that she could feel his growing arousal against her.
'You are the light of my life, *cara.* I love you to complete
and utter distraction. Haven't you realised that yet?'

Her eyes misted over with tears, then she flung her
arms around his neck. 'Oh, Luca. I love you, too.'

His heart turned over, pleasure filling him. 'How
does a honeymoon in Rome sound?'

She beamed him a smile that made his head spin. 'I
think it sounds wonderful. But are you sure you want
to go back?'

He nodded. 'It's time I put the past behind me. You
can help me build new memories.' He lifted her hand to
his mouth and kissed the inside of her wrist. 'Now, let's
go home, *cara.* I've been without you for a week and
it's killing me.'

Morgan laughed. 'We can't go just yet.'

Luca scowled. 'Why not?'

She gestured towards the door. 'Stefania—'

'Will forgive us for leaving when she hears that we are
getting married. She will be in her element, helping you
to arrange the wedding. Where my sister is concerned I've
been blinkered about a lot of things,' Luca added thought-
fully. 'But not any more. She has a husband, he can look
after her in future. I'll be too busy looking after you.'

Morgan snuggled closer. 'And just how do you plan on doing that?'

He fed his hands into the hair on either side of her head. 'Oh, I'll think of something.'

She grasped a handful of his shirt and pulled him even closer. 'And if you can't then I'm sure we can come up with something together.'

Luca bent his head and kissed her. It was a kiss of promise and faith and so, so much more.

He'd been determined his will would prevail. But he'd been wrong about that, too. It was love that was going to prevail...until the end of time.

"YOU HAVE MADE him proud," he told her, nodding at her father, feeling benevolent. "You are the jewel of his kingdom."

Finally, she turned her head and met his gaze, her sea-colored eyes were clear and grave as she regarded him.

"Some jewels are prized for their sentimental value," she said, her musical voice pitched low, but not low enough to hide the faint tremor in it. "And others for their monetary value."

"You are invaluable," he told her, assuming that would be the end of it. Didn't women love such compliments? He'd never bothered to give them before. But Gabrielle shrugged, her mouth tightening.

"Who is to say what my father values?" she asked, her light tone unconvincing. "I would be the last to know."

"But I know," he said.

"Yes." Again, that grave, sea-green gaze. "I am invaluable, a jewel without price." She looked away. "And yet, somehow, contracts were drawn up, a price agreed upon and here we are."

There was the taint of bitterness to her words then. Luc frowned. He should not have indulged her—he regretted the impulse. This was what happened when emotions were given reign.

"Tell me, princess," he said, leaning close, enjoying the way her eyes widened, though she did not back away from him. He liked her show of courage, but he wanted to make his point perfectly clear. "What was your expectation? Do not speak to me of contracts and prices in this way, as if you are the victim of some subterfuge," he ordered her, harshly. "You insult us both."

Her gaze flew to his, and he read the crackling temper there. It intrigued him as much as it annoyed him—but either way he could not allow it. There could be no rebellion, no bitterness, no intrigue in this marriage. There could only be his will and her surrender.

He remembered where they were only because the band chose that moment to begin playing. He sat back in his chair, away from her. *She is not merely a business acquisition,* he told himself, once more grappling with the urge to protect her—safeguard her. *She is not a hotel, or a company.*

She was his wife. He could allow her more leeway than he would allow the other things he controlled. At least today.

"No more of this," he said, rising to his feet. She looked at him warily. He extended his hand to her and smiled. He could be charming if he chose. "I believe it is time for me to dance with my wife."

Indulge yourself with this passionate love story that starts out as a royal marriage of convenience, and look out for more dramatic books from Caitlin Crews and Harlequin Presents in 2010!

TWO CROWNS, TWO ISLANDS, ONE LEGACY

A royal family torn apart by pride and its lust for power, reunited by purity and passion

Harlequin Presents is proud to bring you the
final installment from The Royal House of Karedes.
As the stories unfold, secrets and sins from the past
are revealed and desire, love and passion war
with royal duty!

Look for:

THE DESERT KING'S HOUSEKEEPER BRIDE
#2891

by Carol Marinelli
February 2010

www.eHarlequin.com

HP12891

LARGER-PRINT BOOKS!

GET 2 FREE LARGER-PRINT NOVELS PLUS 2 FREE GIFTS!

HPLP10

PREGNANT BRIDES

*Inexperienced and expecting,
they're forced to marry!*

Bestselling Harlequin Presents author

Lynne Graham

brings you the second story
in this exciting new trilogy:

RUTHLESS MAGNATE, CONVENIENT WIFE
#2892
Available February 2010

Also look for

GREEK TYCOON, INEXPERIENCED MISTRESS
#2900
Available March 2010